THIS DREAM CALLED DEATH

A novelzine by **Stephen Janis**

Published by Novelzine, Baltimore, MD
Cover Photo: Stephen Janis
Layout/Design: Michael Hilton
Copy Edited: Sara Michael

I work for the bureau of dreams in the city of Balaise.

I am a reviewer of waivers assigned to district four, sector three.

My office has space for only two desks: mine and Herman Reel's.

Reel is the director of intake, my supervisor. He is tall, lurching and flatulent and prone to tuck dull colored ties beneath the fold of his belt.

I sit behind a plated metal desk held together by rust. Only one window, a small portal filled with yellow safety glass, allows natural light to enter the room.

When the sun fails to show, which is often in Balaise, I work under the twittering glare of a fluorescent light bulb that hangs from the ceiling like an incurious glow worm.

By late afternoon, on this day, the day of my fifth anniversary with the bureau, Reel slumped over his desk, asleep on the scraps of an unfinished meal.

I, however, continued to pore over the paperwork of errant dreamers.

My job is to review, score, then approve - or deny - the requests for waivers by citizens of Balaise who are scheduled to be remanded to the Waking Recidivist Complex.

I read every waiver filed in my sector.

Some are ketchup-stained forms filled out with scrawled handwriting and littered with indiscriminate spelling errors. Others are neatly typed and precisely worded. All, as required by law, contain a synopsis of the dream, a recommended course of treatment, and a prognosis.

When I am done, if the case merits review, I hand it over to Reel.

"My son didn't dream about death," said a broad eyed, elderly black woman with shock gray hair sitting in front of Reel's desk later that afternoon.

"According to the Bureau enforcement, it was both severe and reoccurring," Reel shot back.

Her eyes flitted toward the ceiling. Her son faced involuntary commitment to the complex for at least a month. Reel was her last hope.

"He's cut back on sleep without even being told," she offered.

Reel pulled out an ink pad, wetted a blotter, and stamped the bottom of her application with his adjutant seal.

"Four hours over 60. Report to the complex by tomorrow noon for dream modification, or I'll issue a warrant."

"But...," she pleaded.

"It is what it is," Reel answered.

Balaise is an old city.

In the morning, the rotten winds sweep embers off the hives of the old industrial sector, blanketing the few skeletal structures downtown that remain erect with a coat of granular soot.

Pollutants, thick with ozone and haze leave the sky without the illusion of sunlight, or a distinct cloud. Just a porcelain gray sheen that glows colorless from light reflected off fragmented stone.

Buildings with gutted facades creep into the middle of the road. Sagging row homes shed paint that drains into culverts, flowing through the alleys like water.

This is Balaise,

I stare out the window of the bus, measuring the grainy patterns of crumbled sidewalk. My left hand drops onto the cold seat just inches from my chest, pushing backwards so my head seems to cascade off the window as the bus bounces over a pothole. I feel weightless.

The sidewalk is slick with rain. Citizens with black umbrellas and hunched shoulders lean into the wind and scramble into alcoves. Black water, acrid rain, cuts through the ancient concrete, carving rivulets into stone and crevices into mortar.

A man sitting in front of me leans his head against the window, then turns to face me.

"I've seen you before," he said.
"Me?" I asked.
"Yes."

Just as his lips part to form another word, the bus stops. I rise from my seat, walk down the aisle, stepping into the muck of unending rain. As the bus accelerates, I see the man mouthing words through the window:

"It is what it is."

My apartment building sits at the bottom of a wide bottomed gully, wrapped in an arterial weave of flagstone sidewalks burnt into the eaves of broken hilltops.

The elevator strains against the heat.

My apartment is small, two rooms, one window and a porcelain bath tub.

The living room floor sags, softened by unrepentant moisture, the byproduct of Balaise's endless humidity.

Two chairs held together with cardboard and glue stand next to a refrigerator. A black lamp shade hangs over my bed.

A single couch stands at a perfect right angle to the window, cushions made of stone.

A mouse grazes on the remains of a carrot stuck in the seams of a wall. My cat watches.

On the book shelf, there is a picture of a child. I glanced at it, as I do every evening. It is a young girl with long straight brown hair and perpendicular smile.

But tonight I work.

A pile of waivers sits on my coffee table. Next to the pile, an advisory,

I light a candle, grab the advisory and read.

To: ALL SECTORS

FROM: THE DEPUTY MAJOR

SUBJECT: DREAM ABOUT DEATH

Advisory No. 9287

BE ADVISED A NEW DREAM ABOUT DEATH HAS BEEN REPORTED. THE CHIEF OF SLEEP RESEARCH IS CURRENTLY CONSTRUCTING A SYNOPSIS FOR GENERAL REVIEW.

ALL EMPLOYEES OF THE BUREAU MUST REPORT ANY NEW DREAMS ABOUT DEATH TO THE BUREAU OF DREAM RESEARCH.

When a new dream about death is reported by enforcement, we are advised. If a citizen confesses dreaming it, remand is automatic.

Yet this advisory was incomplete. There was no synopsis, no narrative, only a vague and incomplete warning.

Still, tomorrow I was confident Reel would get his hands on it.

I said good night to the picture of the girl, as I always did, hoping my dreams would be of her.

In the morning, Reel called.

"Stop by the complex and pick up the advisory on this new dream about death No. 9287," he barked into the phone.

The complex is the largest building in Balaise, the place where all errant dreamers are fixed.

Orange turrets flame above the corners of the glass sided building mottled with brick. Tall arching columns that phase into a spindly web of pneumatic tubing wind up and down walls of stainless steel.

The building is as tall as it is wide. A medieval castle striated with cables.

Inside I locate the central service desk.

"I'm a recorder of waivers, district 3, sector 4."

The desk sergeant checks my ID.

"Yes," he said.
"I'm here to pick up a secure synopsis on dream No. 9287."
"Wait here," he said.

I sat down in a plastic chair soldered to an iron bar.

The sergeant returned.

"9287 is still classified."
"But I received an advisory to report the dream. How can I do that without the synopsis?"
"Orders of the deputy major himself," he snapped.

Later:

"Did you get the advisory?" Reel asked while picking over the terrain of a massive bagel with a rusty knife.
"The synopsis is classified," I said, sifting through the morning pile of waivers.

Reel flipped the bagel over, covering the edges with cream cheese.

"It is what it is," Reel said.

During the bus ride home, a sleeper appears in the middle of the street.

He was lying face up in the middle of Founders Boulevard. The bus driver slammed on the brakes. Several riders were thrown into the aisle.

Exiting the bus, I fumble for my identification.

The sleeper is a gray haired black man with wrinkled skin. His sloping nose spreads along his face like a Sheffield. His deep set eyes are covered with sweat. The bus driver pokes at his head with his foot.

I pull out my ID.

"I'm from the bureau. Step back."

The driver glances at my ID, then complies. I grasp the man's hand and bend over his body as his eyelids flutter.

"Hurry, call it in. I think it's about death."

The driver turns pale then sprints back towards the bus. The sleeper's head rolls from left to right like an epileptic doll. His hands are shaking. For a second he stops breathing. His skin turns light brown. He coughs violently before gasping for air.

He is taken by wagon to the complex.

Later, I am sitting on my couch. I think of him.

Unconscious sleepers were not an uncommon sight in the city. I had personally discovered my fair share of catatonic "errants" - their twitching bodies prone on top of sidewalks, fluttering eyelids frantic as moths. The bureau has taught us to be professional, and usually I am.

Except for the dreams about death.

Death dreams are different. Violent, sometimes convulsive, always unnerving, and at worst a threat to the order and safety of the people of Balaise.

My cat sleeps on the window sill. The city is quiet. I fall into a dreamless sleep, the picture of the girl traced onto the back of my eyelids.

In the morning, Reel calls.

"Stop by district intelligence and pick up the synopsis of the goddamn dream No. 9287."

Housed in the basement of an old firehouse, the Sector Bureau of Dream Intelligence is a labyrinth of file cabinets, shelves stuffed with aging yellowed tablets, and cream colored index cards splayed across monochrome tables.

"I have an inquiry," I told the desk sergeant.
"ID?" he asked, glancing at it for only a second.
"Yes?"
"Dream No. 9287. I need the synopsis."

The sergeant hesitated, unblinking eyes fixed upon me.

"You'll have to see the director. He's in the back."

I walk past a dozen rows of barren shelves. A dismounted globe of the earth sits inert beneath a chair. Behind the last row of shelves is the director's office.

The director is bearded. He wears gold spectacles.

"Yes," he said, without looking up.
"Dream No. 9287. Any update on the advisory?"

He closes a file.

"And you are?"
"Recorder of waivers in this sector," I said.

He picked up a pen, opened a drawer, and handed me a piece of paper.

"At the moment, we have no new information on 9287," he said.
"Has it appeared in this sector?"
"As I said, we have no information," he repeated as he passed the paper across the desk.

"If you fill out this request for special clearance, I'll send it up the chain of command."

The application was blank except for three lines: Name, employee ID and dream number.

"Give it to the desk sergeant," he said.
"I don't understand."
"Deputy major's orders," he snapped.
"It's unusual not to give us the secure synopsis. I am the recorder of waivers."
The director stared at me without blinking.
"It's not unusual for the deputy major to give orders, and in this case he has."

The director lowered his head, opening a file folder sitting on his desk.

"It is what it is," he said.

"Have you heard about the new dream?"

I was startled by the sound of a feminine voice. Dropping the tablet onto my lap, I raised my eyes from the dream blotter.

"Have you heard about it?" a young woman asked.

She was pretty: a lean body in a plain black dress vented at the sides, pallid but smooth skin, glistening teeth and slender hands.

I was sitting on a bench. It was my lunch break.

The bench sat in the middle of an abandoned lot overrun by knotted grass and rat holes.

"Why ask me?"

"We're a stone's throw from the bureau. I thought you would know." she said as she sat down.
"Bad assumption," I answered.

I picked up the tablet.

"Dream blotter," she asked.
"Yes."
"I read it everyday."

I folded the paper and offered it to her.

"Have my copy."
"Like I said," she replied, gently tugging at the end of the tablet.
"I read it everyday."

A pigeon landed in an oily puddle a few feet from the bench. Diesel exhaust from a passing bus spread a cloud of smoke.

"You're interested in dreams?" I asked.
"What else is there to think about in Balaise?"
"Lots of things. That's why we have the bureau. We dream..."
"So you don't have to," she said, finishing the bureau's motto with a chuckle.

Another bus passed. The sun skidded over a hedgerow.

Her skirt was short, revealing a single ivory thigh.

"Do you for work for the bureau?" she asked.
"Yes," I admitted, hoping to extend my view of her leg.
"I am the recorder of waivers in this sector."
"So then you've heard about the new dream."
"No, I haven't."

There was a moment of silence. Her thigh was bone white and skinny.

"It's a dream about death, I hear," she said in a whisper.
"I wouldn't know."
"Please, you do."

"There are bad dreams every day in Balaise, Miss," I answered. "A dream about death rarely stands out."
"But this one," she replied. "This one is different."

The sun caught her hair in spots, refracting black waves of light that blurred my vision.

"How so?" I asked, curious.
"I don't know. I just sense it," she answered.

She stood up, grabbed the tablet and stuffed it under her arm.

"Let me know if you hear anything about the dream," she said as her black shoulder length hair dazzled in the wind.

"You can find me at The Hovel. I'm there every night."

After lunch I counted.

By noon, 392 waivers reviewed, 390 errant dreamers remanded to the Waking Recidivist Complex.

Yesterday 356 waivers reviewed, 354 errant dreamers remanded.

It was an unusually high tally.

For as long as I can remember, 100 waivers comprised an average day's work.

"I don't understand," I said to Reel as he typed furiously. "Why so many?"
"Maybe it's the blacks," he snapped.

Later, Reel, took his frustration out on an appellant.

"Three over 30," he yelled at a young black man with an expansive afro. The rail thin teen slouched in the chair. All I could see was the top of his hair.

"Three over 30. Three over 30," Reel repeated as he lowered his seal like a guillotine onto the waiver.

"That's bullshit. This is bullshit. I didn't fucking dream man. You're making this shit up," the applicant said, his head defiantly aligned with the top of Reel's desk.

"Three hours for thirty days, home monitored and certified. Otherwise I send you to the complex." Reel said.

"But why?"

"Why?" Reel stammered. "Why? Because you had a dream about conveyance, about stealth, about theft. That's why. Because you're thinking negatively, and it's clearly written on your official bureau record, so I can't just let you walk. That's why."

Raising his head, the young man whispered.

"Why?"

I was tired, the apartment hot. A stack of waivers still unprocessed sat on the coffee table.

Sitting on the couch, I stared out the window. Black as death, the night, not a sound from the street - unsettling.

I was thinking about No. 9287, the odd dream about death of which I knew nothing. Why would it be concealed from me? Was it too extreme? Unthinkable?

But who really understood the bureau?

Only the deputy major, I imagined. He made it clear from the moment he took office.

On his inauguration day, humidity dripped like sweat from the sky.

His supporters gathered in front of City Hall at dawn touting coolers filled with Harbor Spring beer and Balasian sausage.

They were a wild bunch: brawlers, thieves, and lawyers - the crusty class of Balaise.

After a lusty morning of drinking, the deputy major finally emerged from City Hall.

Thick, broad shoulders, a strong jaw, an arching forehead dusted with a wild crop of dark black hair and manicured sideburns. He looked like a cartoon hero.

As he strode across the plaza, the crowd erupted into a wild cheer.

Springing onto a makeshift stage, he stood at the podium, his back straight, shoulders thrown backwards. At his side a comely wife and several fidgety children. As the crowd cheered, he raised his left hand in clenched fist.

"This is no time for a celebration," he said, quieting the crowd.

"In fact in my first act as mayor I am declaring a state of emergency."

"A state of emergency born of the reality that Balaise is sick - a dying patient in need of surgery."

"And Balaise is dying," he continued, "because she is not safe."

"And if we are not safe, then we are not whole. Therefore I am not a mayor, but a man whose only job is to guard and advance the interests of the honest, hard-working, -law-abiding - citizen."

"I am not your mayor, I am your deputy major," he said as the crowd cheered wildly.

A black banner began to unfurl from the stanchions of City Hall, a banner as wide as the building itself. It blanketed high arched windows, the pigeon infested vestibules, and obscured the silted sandstone and the crumbling seams of limestone statues.

It was so large that, all of City Hall, the most distinctive looking building in Balaise, became faceless, an ominous black shrine, blind and muted.

As the banner unrolled it scraped the ground. The deputy major turned away from the podium and began waving his arms.

"This is our motto," he proclaimed. "This is how we will change the fortunes of this great city."

BE CONSCIOUS

The crowd erupted again. Wild cheers filled the empty canyons of downtown. The deputy major waved from the podium triumphant, discarding his jacket and tie, donning a military style vest blanketed with epaulets.

The sleeper was stuck in the most uncomfortable position I'd ever seen.

His legs parted in a ballerina's pirouette, the other half of his body submerged inside a large rectangular standing freezer.

I stared, unable to move. A small group of shoppers stood frozen in their tracks too while a man in a brown over coat gingerly touched the sleeper's feet.

"Don't touch him," I said. "I'm from the bureau."

"But I'm the manager, and I need him out of my freezer," the man in the brown overcoat replied.

The sleeper's legs were splayed, his left foot twisted unnaturally.

We are instructed as employees to never move a sleeper. Sudden motion can cause inadvertent movement.

But this man, so oddly positioned, compelled me to act. Forcing myself into the freezer, I pulled out several dozen packages of frozen vegetables pressed against his body. I then placed my left arm around the base of his neck. Prodding his head free, he rolled onto the floor.

He was a young man with short, dark, thick hair, an arched forehead, razor stubble and the stench of aftershave. His eyes fluttered and then opened.

"Where am I?" he asked.
"At the grocer."

He raised a hand to dim the glare of fluorescent lights.

"What was the dream?" I asked.
"I..."

I repeated the question.

"What was the dream?"

He scrambled to his feet.

"Dream?" he asked.
"It's against the law not to report it, all of it."

I could hear the sirens of the bureau sound softly, still distant. Rubbing his brow, the young man nearly whispered.

"Dream?"
"Yes, what was the dream?"

"That it isn't a dream," he said.
"I don't understand?"

"It's about the worst sort of dream there is," he said, scanning the aisles.

"Tell me more."
"No," he answered. "I have to leave."

As shoppers watched, he jumped to his feet, calmly walking down the aisle, never looking back.

Later my apartment is so quiet I could hear the mice curse. I do not watch the dailies or the freak shows. My view box is too old to pick up the new stations.

My only company is the picture of the girl. I think about her, why she disappeared, the freckles on her forehead.

Her picture is a memory of sorts. But there is something about her I cannot remember. Where is she? Does she still live in Balaise?

A pile of waivers wrestles with dust, awaiting my review. But I choose not to work.

I decided to seek company, the woman I met in the park.

In Balaise, one of the remnants of our decline – are hovels. Bars burrowed into basements of aging row homes. Accessible only from alleys, gloomy pits, candle lit, dives submerged below street level. Subterranean hang outs full of smoke and over proof liquor.

The Hovel, the first of its kind, was more than 100 years old.

Buried deep beneath a guttered alley on the East side, The Hovel was carved into the ground like a cave. With a door the size of a manhole, low ceiling and brick walls, it was unnervingly compact, almost claustrophobic.

It was pitch black inside, or nearly so, as I stumbled to a table. I lit a match then a candle – the only lighting available. I ordered a scotch on the rocks served with a warm beer, the Hovel "duo."

The Hovel was packed. Patrons I could see under the cover of darkness wore black – black trousers, silk ties, but in most cases dark leather vests, pants and pull over tops embroidered with spikes, virtual tattoos and dreamland insignias.

Seeking Sylvia, I lifted a candle off my table, and rotated the flame. In a far corner, I spotted a woman, same build, similar hair style. It was she.

"You found me," she said as I approached.
"Yes."
"Odd, isn't it?" she said.
"What?"
"9287."

I studied her face, its furrows and laugh lines. Darkness, though, veiled her eyes.

Who would know, I wondered, the number of a dream? A leaked advisory? Doubtful. Paperwork in the wrong hands? Even less likely. But the woman sitting in front of me was in possession of a number – the number of a dream.

"Who are you?" I asked.
"Honestly," she said, pausing for moment. "I am a reporter for the tablet, the Daily Star."
"The tablet – is that a joke?" I asked, searching again for a facial expression, a raised eyebrow.
"No, it's not."

She touched my hand.

"I've been hearing about this dream, from everyone."
"9287?" I asked.
"Yes."
"I am a recorder of whaivers, not a press liaison."
"I know," she said. "That's why I'm talking to you."
"They'll fire me," I said.

Sylvia placed a notebook on the table. She handed me a piece of paper.

"A gesture of good faith," she said.

It was a bureau advisory.

"How did you get this?" I asked, incredulous.
"I can't tell you," she answered.

To: Deputy Major

From: Director Passel, Chief of Dream Research

Dream About: Death No. 9287

Time: 0700

Dream was reported after an extraction unit from the Bureau of Specialized Enforcement conducted a raid of an alley on the 4800 block Sojourner Avenue at approximately 0800 hours on the seventh day of the third month.

During routine surveillance officers witnessed several white male sleepers in an alley in an area known for negative dreaming. The officers then awoke and questioned said sleepers.

The dreamers were separated and questioned. Dreamers gave conflicting stories and were transported to the Waking Recidivist Complex for further examination.

After intense questioning and waking remediation one of the dreamers, a 29-year-old white male described the dream:

"I was riding a bus somewhere in the city. It was a cold raining day. I noticed two things: everyone on the bus was asleep, and everyone on the bus was black....

"Is that it? Do you have more?" I asked.

Sylvia shook her head.

"No more. I was hoping you could fill in the blanks."
"They won't release the 9287 synopsis."
"Is that unusual?" she asked.
"Yes."

The synopsis was gently withdrawn from my hand.

"It's an odd dream," I said.

Picking up a pen, Sylvia started to take notes.

"Are you quoting me?"

Lifting the pen from the paper, Sylvia jabbed the ball point at my face.

"You help me, I help you. No quotes. All background. Agreed?"
"I'm not sure."
"So it's unusual?"
"Interracial dreams are highly unusual, in fact..."

I paused.

"Yes?"
"Whites rarely dream at all, at least not negatively."
"Most of the dreamers you supervise are black?"
"In my sector, yes."

She wrote furiously now, skipping lines with an erratic cursive, bold strokes nearly illegible.

"And whites rarely dream negatively?" she asked.
"Particularly when it comes to death."
"How rare is it?" she asked, looking up from her notebook.

For a moment, I thought I was staring at the face of child. Only the gentle curve of her eyebrows, thick and dark, suggested a grown woman.

"Almost never," I said.

She smiled, extending her hand across the table. I could feel her fingertips slide between crevices of my hand. The din of the bar turned mute, the desolate smoke thick as a storm cloud.

The touch of her fingers quieted my doubts. We sat peacefully in silence for as long as I could stand it.

The next morning there was not an empty seat on the bus. I stood in the isle bunched up like a grape. A hangover turned into full body nausea. The ride to work was miserable.

As the city uncoiled its shallow sidewalks and tattered billboards, the hollowed skyline looked weary. Old, broken, and mangled, Balaise was indeed a town accustomed to decay.

The deputy major had promised to fix Balaise by fixing our dreams. He said so in a speech a month after he was elected.

All city employees were summoned to Founder's Hall, a giant public mausoleum that housed portraits and the city's historic artifacts: Massive paintings of the harbor splayed neatly on a tide of green grass. Giant hulking cannons firing streaks across the sky into enemy frigates engulfed in flames.

Striding across the stage, the deputy major wore his military uniform he donned the day of his inauguration, now adorned with a svelte blue cape that he cast aside like a prop as he lingered along the front of the stage.

As he reached the podium, wild applause broke out, reverberating through the cavernous room. Before uttering a word, he scanned the audience, his eyes reduced to furtive slits. Then he spoke.

"We are a city under siege," he said.

"We are a city under attack - without safety, a city without a future," he said.

"To turn the tide, to reverse the decline of the great city of Balaise, we must begin to believe again."

The deputy major bowed his head.

"There are some among us, however, who think dark thoughts. Those that want us to fail."

Pointing his finger towards the ceiling, the deputy major's face turned pale. Clenched fists, he pounded the podium.

"We will not allow the naysayers, the negatives, and the critics deprive us of victory. We will not allow those to roam free whose only mission is to stop the citizens of this great city from rising again. We will not allow the corrupt, the malevolent, the partisans of evil still infecting the body of a once proud city to remain."

"Today I declare war on those who do not believe, and I am offering you – the workers that have kept this city alive – the chance to join me on the front lines, the chance to fight the battle with me. I ask you to come with me on this crusade to save the greatest city on earth."

The hall was silent.

A henchman of the deputy major standing at the side of the stage began to applaud. The audience joined in.

As we clapped, hundreds of steel blue handbooks were passed down the aisle, hand to hand, to every worker assembled in the hall. On it, written in bold white letters.

The Balaise Bureau of Dreams

"We dream so you don't have to."

It began, with one, then two.

An administrator in vehicle maintenance. A purchasing manager in fleet services. One by one they left, and those who remained behind worried they might soon be out of a job.

Three months after the deputy major's speech, several of my colleagues and hundreds of other workers had joined the Bureau of Dreams.

Scared I would soon work in a department closed to provide funding for the expansive Bureau of Dreams (the deputy major had already shuttered several small agencies like animal control to fund the bureau's growing budget) I attended an orientation seminar for city employees interested in joining Balaise's fastest growing bureaucracy.

"You have to understand, the dream bureau is like no other government agency in the country," said Alberto Fran, a round, short and heavily whiskered human resources technician. His lodestone eyes looked freakish, offset by wide purple suspenders and madras bow tie.

"We are re-inventing government," he said.

The function of the bureau, explained Fran, was simple in theory.

"To change the fortunes of Balaise you have to change the mind-set of the people, he said, displaying a puffy, medicated grin.

"If we identify negative feelings and thoughts and offer therapy, proactive counseling, then we can properly apply psychiatric assistance to improve our mind set before we get into deeper shit."

"That's why we will focus on dreams. All trouble begins in our unconscious."

Fran explained that the deputy major was a bit of a Jungian – and a philosopher. As a student, and later a member of the city council, the deputy major developed a theory he believed would save Balaise.

"It's called the broken spirit theory," Fran explained. "If you allow the psychological health of a community to deteriorate, than other social ills follow."

"The deputy major has concluded that certain citizens of Balaise are hopelessly negative, and he intends to fix them."

The theory too was simple, Fran assured us. Fix the minor mental disturbances – the petty depression, the temporary trauma – and the general mental attitude of the population and other social ills will improve too. Criminal behaviors, drug addiction, thievery all decline as citizens change their attitudes, improve their mental health, and in the end, believe.

The task of the bureau was to cure the bad dreams of the citizens of Balaise.

"We must convince the people their collective nightmare is over. That is our task."

The city will be divided into nine districts, Fran explained.

Each district will have a bureau outreach center, where citizens could receive free counseling, report their unhealthy dreams, and seek dream repair services to moderate negative or destructive thoughts.

"We're seeking counselors, security, and administrative staff. This is the front lines where any ambitious Balaisian ought to be."

I applied for the latter. Two weeks later I joined the Bureau of Dreams.

The next morning, the pile of waivers sitting on my desk was the highest I'd ever seen.

"They keep coming and coming, I can't stand it," Reel yelled. "I told you the fucking blacks were out of control."

Reel handed me an envelope stamped with seal of the Council of Non-Prophets.

"Arrived this morning by messenger," he said.

I opened it.

You are hereby summoned by the President of the Council of Non-Prophets to appear at a hearing before the non-prophet special investigations committee at 3 p.m. - Tuesday....

"I've been summoned," I said.

Reel rose from his desk and ripped the letter out of my hand.

"Why?"
"I have a no idea. It doesn't say."
"You have too much fucking work to be wasting time sitting in front of the goddamn council answering questions."

Reel snatched a glazed donut out of a paper bag, placing it on top off a folder file.

"I can't just ignore it," I said.
"I would. I would in a minute," he replied, lighting the cigarette. "Grow some balls."

By noon I had assembled the waivers into a neat stack rising nearly a foot off my desk.

"678," I said
"678, what?" Reel barked.
"678 waivers in the morning batch, an estimate based solely on the height of the stack."
"Are you shitting me?"

Reel took a deep drag from him cigarette before burying the butt into a day old aluminum tray of petrified pasta.

"You reject every fucking one of them," Reel stammered. "Reject every fucking waiver. I don't want to see anymore sniveling, watery eyed blacks in my office the rest of this week."
"I can't do that, it's against the law," I replied.
"The law, the law?," Reel repeated. "This is Balaise, we don't have laws, we have people like me. Now you reject them. Otherwise I'll go crazy, and you don't want to see me crazy."

Reel picked up a donut and tossed it at the portal. Bouncing off the glass, the donut hit the ground, spun in a circle and came to rest a few inches from my feet.

"You don't want to see me crazy. Period."

Hours later, Reel sat at his desk typing furiously.

Working non-stop without a break since morning I had managed to get through only half the pile of waivers on my desk.

But as I reviewed a synopsis for a dream about theft, the messenger appeared.

"I've got more," he quipped.
"Go away," Reel yelled.

The messenger shrugged and left them by the door.

Reel pulled a piece of paper from the printer, dislodging his stomach from underneath his desk, exiting the office with unusual agility.

"I'm not going to be a doormat for command...," was all I heard as he walked out the door.

Outside the office, I lugged my briefcase bulging with unprocessed waivers towards the bus stop.

"Got anything?"

It was Sylvia, suddenly walking beside me, the leather notebook in hand.

"Are you nuts? I can't be seen with you."

On the bus, Sylvia handed me a memo.

"Dreams are up, all sectors. Or didn't you know?"

To: Bureau Chiefs, All Sectors

From: The Office of the Deputy Major

Re: Waivers

Significant increases in waiver requests are being reported throughout all sectors, and I have been informed that certain sector commanders believe the unanticipated volume is creating a backlog.

Let me assure all members of the Command Staff the volume of waivers is not unplanned or anomalous, rather it is the result of several command initiatives to compel citizens to report dreams on a more consistent basis.

These initiatives are in response to reports of increased levels of negativity in certain neighborhoods and are only temporary.

We suggest that all sector chiefs review waivers approved for hearings, and if possible encourage sector employees to deny as many requests for waivers as possible. In the short term this should help both alleviate the back log and reinforce the message to the citizens of Balaise that their cooperation in making the city safer is necessary and inevitable.

Sincerely,

DEPUTY CHIEF OF STAFF TO THE DEUPTY MAJOR

"What initiative?, Do you know?" Sylvia asked.
"No."

The bus flinched as it turned onto Founder's Boulevard, coughing up a cocktail of toxins and carbon.

"You owe me twice now," she said. "By the way, did you read the story?"
"What story?"

Sunlight parsed by the dirt encrusted window cast Sylvia's hair a dark jubilant black. Her scent, soft, particular, and vanilla, neutralized the stench of sweat and oil mixed together in the poorly ventilated bus.

For a moment, the smell was enough. Balaise coughed up every noxious odor and industrial waste it could muster, but it all succumbed to Sylvia's scent.

"What story?" I asked.

Again she smiled, her face partially hidden in the filaments of dust, polished by smog and particulate sunlight. Half of her lip curdled into a fluent semi-circle, glazed teeth, minted breath.

What story?" I asked again.

But she did not speak. Instead, she moved closer, her hand laid partially over mine. A leg, uncovered and warm, entangled in my ankle. She gently leaned her body against my shoulder, the full warmth of woman, frail and stimulating.

"Who leaked this to the tablets?"

Standing at the podium in the center of the chambers of the Council of Non-prophets, I had a clear view of Sylvia's article projected upon a screen.

"Are you at all concerned, as an employee of the bureau about the rather negative implications of this headline?" asked Lucinda Curry, president of Balaise's legislative body.

"No," I answered.

"A headline that says: 'Source: Blacks remanded ten times more than whites' – You do not find that disturbing?"

Curry's eyes, polar green ice caps wielded like lasers, were fixed upon me.

"Not really."
"Not really? Explain!"
"If the story is accurate, than I don't find it disturbing," I said.

Craning her neck, adjusting her bifocals, Curry, read:

"According to confidential sources inside the bureau, white citizens of Balaise rarely dream negatively. And blacks, despite rarely reporting their dreams, are more likely to be under supervision of the bureau for sleep restrictions."

Curry shook her head in an odd semi-circular jerk - then reoriented her gaze towards me.

"You don't find that disturbing at all?"
"Not if it's true," I answered.
"And do you know the writer, Sylvia Shunt?"

The council chambers were silent. The 11 members focused intently on Lucinda.

"No, I don't know a Ms. Shunt," I said.
"Are you sure?"
"Yes."

Curry scowled.

"Well then, we have a dilemma. Who from the bureau is leaking this incendiary information to the tablets?"
"I wouldn't know, Madame President."
"You know you're under oath."
"Yes," I replied.

An aide appeared over Curry's shoulder, whispering in her ear. After several minutes of conferring the aide disappeared.

"You don't have any idea?" she repeated.
"No," I answered.
"You've never spoken Sylvia Shunt?"
"No," I repeated.

Curry paused, glaring at me.

"Report to the bureau's Internal Investigation Unit for further questioning. Understood?"
"Yes Madame President."
"You're excused. This meeting is adjourned," she said sharply, rapping the almond-shaped gavel on her desk. Dismounting the dais, Lucinda hurriedly walked towards the exit, eyeing me warily.

On the bus to the Waking Recidivist Complex to the Office of Internal Affairs, I recalled with some bitterness that my testimony before the council was not my first encounter with Lucinda.

Nearly a year before her appointment as president of the Council of Non-prophets, a student in a middle school chemistry class plucked a large thermometer from off the wall and hurled it a rival.

Striking the wall just inches from a substitute teacher, the thermometer shattered, releasing a pool of mercury large enough to kill everyone.

The fire department evacuated the school, but the classroom was unusable.

Following city procedure I put the job out for bid, placing an advertisement in the tablets. Six companies responded, and the lowest bidder won the job.

But just days before work was scheduled to begin, a woman appeared in my office unannounced. She wore a dark blue blazer and gray pants. Her shoulders were relatively broad for a woman. A streak of white hair ran down the left side of her head. She looked like a lesbian skunk.

Before I could say a word, she began to scream.

"You screwed us! You really screwed us!"
"Who are you?" I yelled back.

"I am Lucinda Curry," she shouted. "I am the executive director of the Society for Chemicals Against Children, and you screwed us."

"I don't know what you're talking about."
"The goddamn mercury spill. That contract should go to us!"
"Lowest bidder wins Ms. Curry," I replied.

Stomping her foot on the floor, Lucinda grabbed the edge of my desk.

"I don't care about procedure, we are a fucking non-profit, and we serve the citizens of Balaise."

"City code is clear, but you're welcome to challenge," I replied.

Unappeased, Lucinda paced in erratic, ever widening circles.

"We - and I mean all non-profits are working on behalf of the people to save this rotten city, so we're in no position to compete with commercial companies. We – exclusively - have the best interests of the children of Balaise as the core of our mission!"

After a half hour of sputtering and cursing from various corners of my office, she exhausted my patience. I promised to give her preferred bidder status for future contracts. But my offer was met with silence, after which she left vowing to go my over head.

And that was, I thought, the end of it.

But a few days later I was summoned to the office of the Director of Purchasing. To my surprise, Lucinda was sitting quietly in a foldout chair, her crystalline green eyes fixed upon me.

"Have a seat," the director said.

"I want to discuss some disturbing allegations made by Lucinda," he added, looking at her before resuming.

"I've known Lucinda for a long time, and I know her to be an honest woman."

Pausing briefly to inhale, the director spread his fingers across his desk, speaking slowly.

"Did you – and I'm only going to ask you once – seek sexual favors from Lucinda in exchange for the contract to clean the classroom?"

Without thinking I laughed.

"Are you serious?"
"Dead," answered the director.

Lucinda lips curled in a precipitous smile, like she was going to jump off a bridge.

"You said if I fuck you, then it was mine. That's it," she added.
"You can't honestly believe her. She's insane," I responded, stunned.
"Lucinda is threatening to go to the tablets, and if she does, who cares if it's true," the director said.

Lucinda smiled, a cursive grin, her seething eyes molten lead. The director stared out the window as he spoke.

"I think we can give her the contract, correct?"

I left the office without saying another word. That afternoon I awarded the job to The Society for Chemicals Against Children.

To this day the classroom is probably still laden with mercury.

But that was not the end of her reign.

Just a year after my first encounter with Lucinda, I was sitting at my desk reviewing waivers, Reel stormed into the office waving a piece of paper.

"You're not going to fucking believe this," he said, clutching a mangled copy of the Daily Star in the air.

"They deputy major disbanded the city council and replaced it with a bunch of do-gooders," he continued, shaking his head.

"The fucking guy is loony."

"How is that possible?" I asked.

"Said here in the tablets he declared a state of emergency," Reel said, reading from the Daily Star.

"In another bold and unexpected move, the deputy major has invoked emergency powers to utilize a little known rule in the city's charter that allows the mayor to disband the city council in 'extreme and extenuating circumstances,'" Reel read scratching his head. "I can't fucking believe it," he said as he continued to read.

"As part of a plan the reform government," Reel read. "The deputy major has convened a new governing body of Balaise, the Council of Non-Prophets," Reel continued.

"His first appointment is Lucinda Curry, president of the Society for Chemicals Against Children," Reel continued. "She will serve as president of the council, Reel read before tossing the paper onto my desk, flailing his arms like an epileptic referee.

"You read the rest. I can believe it. That bitch will ruin this city," Reel said, opening the top drawer of his desk and removing a package of jelly crumpets.

"He's lost his mind. He's lost his fucking mind," Reel repeated as I reread the article, a knot of clay expanding in my stomach with each successive word.

"The people who run the city's non-profits are the true heroes," the deputy major was quoted. "We need their wisdom to move his city forward."

Reel continued his flow of curses muddied by a mouthful of confectionary sugar. I sat at my desk, unable to process a waiver for the rest of the afternoon.

The Internal Investigations Unit of the bureau occupies the entire top floor of the Waking Recidivist Complex.

The desk sergeant directed me to the special elevator tucked in the corner of an emergency stairwell. It was a plain steel box, bereft of floor numbers, a pneumatic tube with smooth inner skin and glistening walls.
The doors shut automatically after I entered. The tube moved with gut-wrenching speed.

Almost as violently as the tube accelerated, it came to an equally violent stop that pitched me face first toward onto the floor.

The doors opened.

I was greeted by a bristled web of blonde hair attached to a short woman with thighs as thick as tree trunks.

"Follow me," she said.

The IIU offices were deserted, poorly lit, the air extremely dry and static. Flat screens, with parched buttons and flashing LED displays, sat blinking on a seemingly endless row of empty oval-shaped desks. A bank of printers mounted on the ceiling dropped reams of paper into steel baskets. The floor was thick with colored cables, tied into bundles, exposed veins and shielded snakes.

Inside an empty conference room, the blonde ushered me into a chair at the end of a long table.

The room was sparsely furnished, no phones or view screens. Dimly lit, wood paneled, the only sign of life: the hum, felt but not heard.

I waited for what seemed like an hour.

Finally two men entered the room, unfamiliar but clean shaven faces, heavily scented, wearing exotic ties and tailored suits.

For several minutes they simply stared at me, perfectly still, not a word, or utterance, until one man with almond eyes and a wafer thin nose, cleared his throat.

"We know," he said as he pulled an envelope from his jacket and placed it on the table.

"We know," he repeated, as his counterpart simply stared at me.

"You lied to the Council of Non-prophets," he said.

Two pictures removed from the envelope were laid end-to-end. One photo depicted me and Sylvia sitting in the park. The next: Our walk to the bus stop.

"We've been following her," the talker said.
"You follow reporters?" I asked.
"Yes," he answered.

The pictures were clear and intimate. Sylvia's untamed hair blown by the wind. The ragged hedges of the park, a wild stalk of grass the back-drop for the Sylvia's odd, thin figure.

"Clearly that's you," the talker added.
"Yes," I said.

The talker clapped his hands, then grabbed the pictures off the table, stuffing them back into the envelope.

"Why did you lie?" he asked.
"Because I hate Lucinda," I answered.

The talker smirked.

"It's not a bad thing, lying to the council; We do it all the time. However, it could be a problem, should the truth ever be revealed," he said, rubbing his eyebrow.

"Are you going to tell them?" I asked.
"Not yet," he said.

The silent man reached into his pocket and produced another envelope. Pushed across the table by the talker, it came to rest directly next to my hand.

"Open it," the talker said.

It was the picture of a black woman –a familiar black woman with a pronounced forehead, simmering eyes. At the bottom of the picture, her name: Jasmine Brown.

"Jasmine Brown?"

The man who had yet to speak added,

"You want to leak stories about blacks, here's your chance," he said.

"Jasmine Brown is the biggest threat to the bureau in Balaise," he began.

"She has spread lies, riled up the blacks, and generally made it impossible for us to operate the program."

"So while the black neighborhoods continue to be the most negative, the only thing Brown seems to be able to do is cause trouble, and worst of all, criticize the deputy major."

"The point is," the less talkative speaker added, "We need to neutralize Brown," he said.

"We need to undermine her credibility."

"Why don't you remand her?" I asked. "Put her in the complex?"

"Too risky without cause," he said pausing.

I studied the dossier. It listed Brown's age, height, last known address. No dream report or bureau profile, just a phone number.

"We need useful information," said the talker. "Something that would be of interest to the tablets – an illegitimate child, a bad habit, debts, a lesbian affair."

"About indecency would be the best case scenario," he added.

The talker stopped, leaned forward and whispered,

"That would be great."
"But I am a recorder of waivers, not an investigator."

The talker grinned. His counterpart chuckled.

"It is what it is."

The bus faltered in the combustible stew of summer smog and intermittent rain. It was an odd combination of heat and precipitation that opened the pores of abandoned buildings, covered my brow with sweat, and mixed sunlight into a glassy, dull gray.

I stopped at Ferey's BBQ, a grand sloping wooden fortress of a restaurant that enveloped an entire block of East side real estate. I ordered a beer and watched the citizens of Balaise crowd the sidewalks in front of a row of take-out windows, hungry and calm, but alert.

Later I simply rode past my stop studying Jasmine Brown's dossier. She was well proportioned, sparkling dark eyes, and no doubt a forceful speaker featured prominently on the nightlies. She was the face of dissent against the bureau. Pumping her fist at a rally, cameras following like a swarm of electric bees. Jasmine, standing on a makeshift podium before hundreds of blacks, seething with anger, the vessel, it seemed to me, of inexplicable hate.

At the bureau, we always regarded her with curiosity. More blacks entered sleep supervision because more blacks dreamed bad thoughts. It was not a matter of prejudice on my part or that of any other person I worked with. Just the result of the bureau working as it was designed. If more blacks dream, and dream badly, then more blacks will have their unconscious thoughts corrected.

But Jasmine did not accept the inevitable logic of cause and effect. She told the tablets the bureau was prejudiced, that dream bureau agents harassed blacks, spied on their community meetings, and filed false dreams reports. She said that blacks were forced to report dreams that never occurred, coerced into seeing dream counselors – all because the deputy major wanted to prove his broken spirit theory worked.

And while the blacks continued to suffer, Jasmine continued to protest. She marched at rallies, wrote editorials, and spoke out on the nightlies against the bureau. Meanwhile the deputy major held firm – the bureau, and his broken spirit theory, would save Balaise. Only Jasmine stood in his way.

And now, because of a reporter named Sylvia, Jasmine Brown was my problem.

The next morning, I met Reel for breakfast.

"You really screwed up big time," Reel said, scanning the menu.
"I didn't tell the council anything that wasn't true," I replied.

Reel picked at his nose as flies gathered on the remains of a gargantuan slice of toast.

"Anyway, I'm not an investigator. I don't know what they expect."
"Nothing," Reel replied. "And they don't care if you are good or bad," he said.
"They got something on you, so when you get your hands dirty, they'll stay dirty," he said.

The early breakfast crowd surged towards the counter. Grim-eyed Balaisians clutched paper bags slick with spilled coffee and donut grease.

A wall-eyed waitress with a rail of adult acne circumcising her chin scrambled between tables, filling coffee cups while spouting expletives.

"Worst case scenario, they hand you over to the council. Best case you give them something to take down Brown," Reel said.

It seemed logical. Thanks to a drink and bus ride with a reporter, I was a perfect, low risk, high reward gambit.

"The thing is," Reel continued, "the deputy major has higher ambitions. And higher ambitions means higher stakes."

"So don't get in his way, do what you have to do, and then disappear."

A fresh bagel arrived with a side of slick sausage and bowl full of donut holes. Knife in hand, Reel attacked.

"Because you see," Reel continued, "the broken spirit theory is his baby. If it fails, his career is over."

The waitress lunged at Reel's coffee cup. Her imperfect body - floundering hips and husky shoulders - spread across the table. A wisp of a mustache traced an odd, erratic curve over her upper lip.

"Anything else Reel?" she asked, winking at me.
"Yea, a side of hash browns, quickly," he said, spanking her as she turned towards the kitchen.

"Best of all," Reel continued, "if you bring down Brown, you'll have something on them.
"And so will I," Reel said, laughing out the side of his mouth.
"That's great," I replied, my appetite suddenly gone.
"My career is over."
Reel smiled.

"It is what it is!"

Later that afternoon a bureau messenger delivered a thick manila envelope.

Inside was my new bureau ID, indentifying me as a community relations specialist, grade III, a black notebook with a packet of blank dream citations, and the phone number for my liaison at the district where Brown lived.

My orders: Travel to Brown's neighborhood and collect "human intelligence of the negative variety." I was to report to the bureau "twice daily" through district headquarters.

I said goodbye to the picture of the girl. I left an extra dish of food for the cat.

As I boarded the bus headed to the West side neighborhood controlled by Brown, I wondered. Five years processing waivers, reviewing thousands of dreams, sitting next to Reel and remanding people to the complex and suddenly I am an investigator? Worse yet, I was now an operative sneaking into a community under the cover of a legitimate job. If the broken spirit theory worked, why bother?

And now I was on an unfamiliar bus. A sea of black faces crammed into every seat with excess passengers standing in the aisle. The thick diesel back draft was twice as stifling. Air-conditioning non-existent, forced to stand shoulder to shoulder with my fellow riders, our arms entangled in a haphazard embrace.

And as the blank darkness of downtown Balaise disappeared, a different type of decay emerged.

Broken row homes dipped, their roofs tilted perpendicular towards the sidewalk. Solid brick buildings were replaced by wood structures, large boarding houses with cracked windows and dirt yards.

Tight brick courtyards gave way to large vacant weed-filled lots, pockets of dust and trash, molting dogs and rats. Barren stretches of naked land were punctuated by a lone structure, a shack wrestled into the ground.

Still, as I watched the neighborhoods roll by from the bus, it was clear blacks had one thing in abundance: people.

Every corner, sidewalk, overgrown park was filled with people. Downtown Balaise was a ghost town. But as the bus drew closer to Brown's territory, the BBQ stands, liquor stores, barbershops and churches housed in abandoned store fronts were bursting with human beings.

Children played in the streets riding stripped down bicycles and miniature motor scooters. Makeshift basketball hoops hung on the window sills of abandoned homes. Small groups of men huddled around stoops throwing dice or sipping of liquor wrapped in brown paper bags.

Brown's neighborhood was the same.

Old men in corduroy hats, teenage boys in wifebeaters, and young mothers pushing strollers milled about the entrance of a church that encompassed two city blocks.

It was a massive building built entirely out of millstone with a steeple that stretched hundreds of feet skyward.

A banner hung across the arched entrance:

This morning, the Honorable Christian Williams, protégé and spokesman for the Honorable Jasmine Brown, will be appearing to call for end to the deputy major's broken spirit policy which is destroying our community. Mr. Williams will speak the truth and you need to hear it!

I flashed my Bureau badge to a man standing at the door.

"Bureau community relations," I said.

The doorman nodded, and I entered.

Inside, the heat was oppressive. Soggy and humid, a bathhouse of solar radiation trapped in the unventilated sanctuary.

The pews were filled with blacks, sweating, napping, and warding off perspiration with improvised paper fans and towels. A low monotone dirge played from an electronic organ. Overheated babies cried out in despair.

As I searched for an empty seat, a tall man wearing a gray pin striped suit approached.

"Mr. Christian would like to see you privately before he speaks. Please follow me," he said.

Lead from the sanctuary to a spiral staircase off the vestibule, I was escorted into a small room with a table, two chairs, and a desk lamp.

"Have a seat," said the man, who quickly left the room.

Ten minutes passed before I heard the rumbling of applause. I tried to open the door, but it was locked.

I sat in the chair and waited, frustrated that I had been duped.

I could hear voices vibrate through the ceiling. Then what sounded like a thousand shoes pounding the floor simultaneously. Finally applause shook the table and rattled the walls.

Almost an hour a passed before the door opened.

"A representative from the bureau, what a wonderful surprise," said a tall, dark skinned man wearing a fluorescent purple paisley tie and a dark tailored suit.

"Christian Williams," he said, sitting down directly across from me.

"I would have liked to hear your speech," I said.
"I'm sure you would have," he answered, as several other tall men, all dark skin and dressed in suits entered the room.

"But it was a private community meeting."
"I work for the bureau's community relations unit. Perhaps I could have added our point of view to yours," I answered. Several men chuckled. Williams joined them with a full belly laugh.

"Of course," he said, taking a cigarette out of a silver case. "Just another helpful person from the bureau," he added, still laughing.

"Now why are you here?" he snapped, his incandescent smile gone, his saucer shaped-eyes suddenly fierce.

"What do you mean?"
"The bureau doesn't have a Community Relations Unit, just fools like you that think they can trick black folks."

The chuckling, laughter, and smiles ceased as Williams leaned over, gripping the bottom of the table and pushing it slightly forward into my chest.

"If you think we're stupid enough to believe you're here to help us, then maybe we're stupid enough make you tell us why you're here."

Williams stared blankly as two members of his entourage moved directly behind me.

"So you can tell us," he said slowly.

"I'm here to be of assistance anyway that I can, Mr. Williams," I replied.

Williams nodded. Two pairs of hands grabbed my shoulders.

"There's no reason for you not to be honest with us," he said.
"You've got nothing to lose," he said

"But I am going to kick your monkey white ass if you don't tell me."

Williams paused as a contrail of smoke streamed from his nose.

"We know what that fucking deputy major wants, and we're not going to give it him."

A nod from Williams, and I felt a sharp stinging pain emanate from the back of my head.

"Jesus, are you crazy? I'm from the bureau!"

"It's nothing more or less than you're doing to us," he replied, stubbing out his cigarette on the table.

"Now, do you want to share?"
"Share what?" I asked.

This time I heard it coming: A cold slap to the skull with the open palm of a large and powerful hand, the force of which drove my head forward and bounced it off the table top.

At first I was stunned, momentarily lost.

"It's odd. Every few months, a community relations worker from the bureau just happens to show up at one of our community meetings."

"Well mannered gentleman like you, always friendly, and inquisitive," Williams said, glancing at his men.

"And of particular interest is our own fearless leader, Jasmine Brown," Williams said.

"And why is that, Mr. Bureau? Why is our beautiful, intelligent, heroine of interest?" he asked.

"I don't know," I answered.

"At the very least, this will give you something to talk about at headquarters," Williams said with a smile.

"Now do we have to do it again?"
"No," I answered.

Williams sat back in his chair, adjusting his tie.

"I'm waiting to hear, in fact, I'm looking forward to it."

But before the unseen hand could deliver another blow, a chorus of screams, high pitched and feminine, filled the building. A stampede of feet pounding the floor shook the ceiling like an earthquake.

William's bodyguards quickly ran out the door, shoving me off the chair as they sprinted into the hallway, Williams in tow.

Left alone, I followed.

I found an emergency stairwell that lead into a courtyard. Following the screams, I navigated through a maze of concrete doorways until I was standing in front of the church.

A dozen black vans with the bureau insignia painted broadly across the side were parked in the street, beacons flashing.

Bureau police, dressed in black sleeveless vests and black body armor stood guard at the church's entrance. Dozens of blacks were standing in a serpentine line, wailing, gesticulating. Guards, with impassive faces and plastic handcuffs slung on their belts, frisked and questioned the blacks scattered across the sidewalk. Another line of blacks, handcuffed and silent, were led one by one into the back of awaiting vans.

"Who the hell are you?" asked a bureau enforcement officer with two gold bars on his collar.

"I'm a community relations specialist," I said, showing him my badge.

"Get in the van," he said sharply.
"Me?"
"You can sit in the front. We're clearing right now."

On the steps of the church, Christian was arguing with one of the guards, gesturing towards the sky.

"You will not get away with this! God as my witness!"

The guard stood silent and expressionless. As I approached, Christian swung around, his eyes bulging with rage.

"You!" he said pointing at me. "You, the stooge, the community relations minion of the bureau, look what you have done to my people!" he said.

Lunging from the steps, Christian extended his hands, reaching for my throat. In an instant, the guard raised a truncheon, striking him in the back of the head.

The blow catapulted him down the steps of the church, his black, sweaty head resting on the tips of my shoes.

Two hands grabbed me by the shoulders. I was dragged, stunned and silent, into a van as the cries of blacks filled the air. I was shoved into the front seat while a nameless driver engaged the engine and sped towards district headquarters.

"We're taking you off the streets," said the short, scrawny and pale district commander.

"You've been exposed," he added.
"I agree," I replied.

"It's not entirely your fault. We've been relatively unsuccessful in penetrating Jasmine Brown's organization," he said, shuffling through a file that I assumed was hers, his thick plasticized glass-es magnifying two cavernous eye sockets.

"The operation, the vans, I didn't know the bureau was..."
"Aggressive," the commander finished.
"Yes."

He stood up, backed away from his desk.

"What the hell did you expect? The goddamn blacks have done nothing but continue fuck things up for both themselves and the deputy major," he said.

"We want to help them, but all they do is complain, accuse and run to the tablets," he continued.

"All we ask is that they report their dreams," he continued.
"Instead they throw cunts like Jasmine Brown at us."

The commander picked up the file, thrusting it in my direction.

"All these reports, Jasmine and her protest, people refusing to file dream reports," he said.

"Meanwhile this neighborhood is a shithole, the worst in Balaise."
"I didn't realize," I replied.
"You work downtown right?"
"Yes."

"Out here, it's the Wild West, and the deputy major is not happy," he said.

"They'll have my ass soon if I don't get this district under con-trol," he said.

"And God forbid I have another heavy month of dreams about death."
"You mean 9287?" I asked.
"Never heard of it," he said.

The phone on his desk rang.

"Yes," he barked. "Hold on."

He handed the receiver across his desk.

"It's for you," he said.

"Don't say a fucking word," Reel said. "There's a pay phone on the corner across from district headquarters. Tell them you need to go to the bathroom, find the pay phone and call me at the office. Don't say anything. Don't ask why, just hang up and ask him where the fucking bathroom is."

I handed the receiver back to the commander.

"Where's the bathroom?"
"Down the hall and to the right," he answered.

As I turned to leave, the commander added,

"Don't take too long. We have an escort van waiting to take you downtown."

It wasn't hard to escape district headquarters. I simply walked out the door.

Across the street, the pay phone stood on the corner exactly as Reel described.

"You're calling from the pay phone, right?"
"What's going on?," I answered.
"They've got you fucking remanded to the complex!" Reel said.
"That's impossible," I replied.
"I'm staring at the paperwork. It says automatic remand to Waking Recidivist Complex for undetermined length of time. Subject identified as dreamer of No. 9287 dream about death and will be incarcerated for treatment by order of the Bureau of Dream Investigations. You're totally screwed," Reel said.
"I don't believe it."

"Believe it, shithead. I'm holding the order in my fucking hand," Reel replied.
"It's just not possible. I remand people, I don't get remanded." I said.

I stood on the corner holding the phone. The bureau district headquarters looked mottled, dull colored and alabaster like an antiquated fun house.

"What the fuck am I going to do," I said, crouching beneath the cast iron clam shell casing that buffeted the phone from the fury of the street.
"Find Jasmine Brown. Get something," he said. "Get some dirt and bring it to me, I'll go to the deputy major myself."
"How the fuck I am supposed to do that?"
"Find her, just find her. You'll get something,"
A bureau van turned onto the street, beacons flashing. I ducked lower, watching it disappear around the corner.
"Lay low and call me when you find something," Reel said.
"And don't go back to the station house. Get lost."

I hung up the phone.

Never in a million years did I expect to find myself facing remand.

Yes I had dreamed, but not negatively. My psych profiles were spotless. My checkups regular. Rarely would a month pass when I wouldn't stop by the employee counselor's office to recount my dreams and share my thoughts. I'm not euphoric and unreasonably unhappy, but I was no more or less sullen than the average Balaisian – hardly a candidate for the bureau's most severe form of therapy.

I crawled around the corner in a crouch to avoid the surveillance cameras that hung from telephone poles like odd, metallic fruit.

Once safely into an alley, I resigned myself to the fact Reel was right. I had to find Jasmine Brown. I didn't know what I was going to do if and when I found her, but I certainly couldn't go strolling back into headquarters. Remand was not an option.

Despite having spent most of my life in Balaise, I knew little about the black neighborhoods. Downtown was my home.

And now, as I crawled from alley to alley, slowly putting distance between myself and district headquarters, I was confronted by unfamiliar street names and foreign landmarks.

Black faces were curious, distant, and sometimes hostile. As I exited the alley, three young men wearing long red t-shirts and low rise jeans huddled next to a stoop.

"I think I'm lost," I said, smiling.

They did not reply.

I found a small convenience store wrapped in iron bars and steel. Through a small hole in urine-colored safety glass I asked a stout Asian woman for directions to Brown's neighborhood.

"I don't know she said, "Buy map."

I purchased a map, unfolding it in the corner of the poorly lit store. Blacks filed in and out, glancing at me as they bought food, liquor and cigarettes.

Balaise is not intuitively organized. Streets start South, turn West, and then collapse into a disorienting ellipses. Boulevards evaporate into narrowing side streets. Broad avenues dwindle into obscure alleys.

Brown's neighborhood was not far, according to the map, but a direct route was intersected with too many bureau checkpoints. So I plotted a path to avoid major streets and trafficked thoroughfares.

Peering around corners, jogging from alley to alley, I was observed like a stray cat or dreaming derelict in search of blast.

But as I edged closer to Brown's territory, Mount Zion, the half-curious stares of the young men congregated on the corners and half-naked women pushing baby strollers turned hostile.

Crossing Mount Avenue, a four lane boulevard thick with hackney cabs and trucks cutting across town, two young men dressed in suits began to follow me, or so it seemed.

Reaching the sidewalk, I spotted the Mount Avenue motel, a two story structure with crumbling balconies and ashen windows. Inside the lobby was enclosed in a thick metal cage, an oblong black speaker mounted on the wall. A voice, sight unseen, spoke.

"What do you want?"
"A room," I said.
"How many people?"
"One."
"Twenty." he said.

A key was slipped through a portal. To my right, a rusted box held a pile of tablets called the Afro-United. I took one.

The room was musty, the walls dotted with a black spotted mold. A clock radio sat on side table. The bedspread was wracked with open sores.

I opened the Afro-Union, and thought for a moment my luck had changed.

Jasmine Brown to speak tonight.

Community activist Jasmine Brown will speak about the harassment of blacks by the Bureau of Dreams at the Woodrow Sandling elementary school this evening at 8 p.m. All residents are welcome to come and learn why the black community of Balaise suffers disproportionately the negative effect of the policies of the deputy major.

There was no better way to get what I needed than to meet Brown in person.

Setting the alarm clock for seven, I drifted off into a light, dreamless sleep.

Later, I do not know much later, something woke me. I turned on the light and raised my head. My eyes still accustomed to the dark could see only the black outlines of what appeared to be a man sitting in the threadbare arm chair next to the window.

"Did I wake you?" It was Christian, his voice unmistakable.
"Yes," I answered.

There was a moment of silence interrupted by the gentle murmur of an electric fan.

"I came to wish you well," he said.
"How did you find me?" I asked.
"We know everything that happens in the Mount, Mr. Bureau," he said, striking a match, the flame outlining the cut line of his jaw.

"I guess I should have expected that," I said.

Christian chuckled.

"I came to wish you well on your death," he said, now laughing.
Startled, I threw of the bed sheet and stumbled onto the floor.

"Don't panic Mr. Bureau, your death will not be at our hands," he said. "It has been pre-ordained. It is in the air. It has been set in motion by the people for whom you work, and will end exactly as they planned it."

"I don't understand," I replied.

"Your deputy major, he is obsessed with death, correct?" he asked.
"I don't know," I replied.

"He talks about it all the time. He conjures it in his speeches, threatens it in his language, and then he speaks of it in dreams."

A gentle stew of cigarette smoke congregated in a cloud over Christian's head. Street lights cast backwards shadows, covering his face with tracers of translucent gray.

"His perfect enemy, the dream about death, the specter that fills the void, so to speak."
"What do you mean?" I asked.

"That's a question for you to answer," Christian said, turning his head towards the window.

"Look at the clock," he said.

I glanced at the clock on the night table. It was plain, digital matchsticks perfectly synchronized, realigning to form numbers.

"Notice anything unusual," he asked.
"No," I answered.
"Look again."

A second glance and it was obvious. The clock was moving backwards, time in reverse.

I picked it up off the table, turned it over and studied the plastic backing, the power cable, the snooze button - nothing unusual.

"There's nothing wrong with it, just a reminder," he said.
"I still don't understand."
'This is your dream," Christian said, rising from the chair. "This is your dream about death."

Clutching the clock in my hands, I searched for the reset button, the plastic cap that allowed seconds minutes and hours to be changed.

"It is simply counting backwards, the time that remains," he said. "It is the same for all of us."

"How did you do it?" I asked watching the seconds retreat, time's arrow move in reverse.

"Like I said before, this is your dream about death," he said.

"It is the same for all of us."

As he turned the door knob, the alarm clock went off, a screeching, intimate digital blast.

And then I woke up. It was 7. I had been dreaming. I had dreamed about death.

The William Willard School was just a few blocks from the Mount Avenue Hotel.

As dusk settled, the fetid humidity turned into a cloying wall of unmovable air. My standard bureau uniform – a white linen shirt, a tie divvied into geometric shapes filled with dull industrial colors – was soaked.

Mount Avenue looked baked. The sun ingested by leftover haze ducked beneath a low ceiling of clouds.

Embroidered cars with shimmering kaleidoscope spokes and turbine carburetors crawled along the street. Groups of young women, lithe bodies stuffed into tight jeans, shimmied on the sidewalks.

The William Willard School was a low slung building.

Sagging windows scraped the ground, cracked brick walls foisted by dull blue metallic pillars. The silver acetone lettering proclaiming its namesake was missing letters. Small piles of trash, compacted beer cans and ragged tablets littered the parking lot.

Security would be tight, so I decided to avoid the front door.

In back of the school piles of trash filled an empty parking lot. A putrid mattress swarmed with rats. Coveys of cockroaches slalomed between discarded tins of rotting fish.

Down a small flight of concrete stairs, I found an open door.

Inside the air smelled moldy. A dangling fluorescent light tube flittered like a firefly.

Navigating between the shadows of old file cabinets and stacks of mildewed books, I spotted a set of stairs. Just as I set foot on the first, a booming voice barked from behind a stack of calcified books.

"What the fuck are you doing?" said the voice.

I ducked down against the wall, crouching on top of a murky puddle.

"Speak," he said.
"Speak," he repeated, stepping into the glare of a twittering strobe light.

An old man, shoulders hunched and specks of a gray beard matched with dazzling portishead eyes, stood just inches from my face.

"I'm trying to find the auditorium," I said, standing up slowly.

He shined the flashlight directly into my face.

"Who are you?"
"I'm to here to see Jasmine Brown speak," I replied.

He wore a black jacket, a tattered white shirt draped down to his knees, and oddly flared blue jeans. His face was peppered with splotches of pinkish skin.

"Jasmine Brown," he repeated, his voice rising in pitch slightly.
"She's speaking in the auditorium tonight," I said.

The man dropped the flashlight.

"Jasmine Brown?" he repeated.

"Yes," I said.

Brushing off his jacket, he turned and walked towards a rusted stairwell.

"Follow me," he said.

Leading me up the stairs, he stopped at the door, speaking with his back turned as he gently tugged on the door knob.

"Why are you're here to see Brown?" he asked. "And why come in the back door?"

"Look at me," I answered without thinking. "Would they let me in the front?"

He shrugged, opening the door before stepping into a dark hallway. "I knew her father."

"They killed him too," he added.

"They didn't kill him with a gun or a knife, but it was murder just the same," he said, his voice echoing through the empty corridors.

"He knew it was going to happen. He even told me so," he said.

"'Don't worry about your dreams,' he told to us before he died," the man said, as he shuffled down the hallway, groping the sides of empty lockers rusted and warped by time.

"But the bureau, the bureau is the worst thing that ever happened to this city. They have no business being in our heads. And they had no business killing Caisson Brown."

Reaching two large metal doors, the man stopped, shaking the steel handles before turning around.

"I still don't understand why you want to see Ms. Brown?" he said, his already gravelly voice dropping several octaves.

"What do you want with Jasmine?"
"I just need to see her," I replied.

The man scowled, his eyes turned gray.

"I'm an old man. I've lived in the basement of this school since the bureau remanded me without cause," he said.

"I never been the same. They sullied my mind," he continued. "Still, I wasn't stupid before they got me, and I ain't stupid now."

"So my question is why sneak in through back of the building to see Ms. Brown with no good explanation?"

I did not answer. I could hear the rumbling of the crowd behind the door, scattered applause, and the booming voice of a preacher reciting what sounded like a prayer.

"I am with the Bureau of Dreams," I said. "Or at least I was,"
"The bureau," he asked, his pupils expanding.
"Yes."
"The goddamn bureau. You can't be for here any good reason," he said, placing his body directly between me and the door.

The booming male voice reached a crescendo.
"I should have known," he continued, spreading his arms across the doors. "I should know you were up to no good."

"I'll admit, that the bureau does not like Ms. Brown," I said. "And I'll even admit they sent me here to hurt her."

I paused.

"But I've left the bureau," I said.

The man shook his head, clenching his hands, thrusting two large fists in front of my face.

"You're lying, it's as plain as day," he said. "You're a goddamn no good two-faced liar."

"Maybe," I said. "Maybe, but I know what they're going to do to her. I know what they have planned. I want to help her."

"The bureau plans to take her down," I added.

"You're lying," the man replied, his fists shaking.
"Why don't we let Jasmine Brown decide that?"

The old man stared. The applause swelled, breaking into a rhythmic cadence. The crowd chanted her name, repeating it like a mantra.

He shook his head.

"I'm going to let you in against my better judgment. Should have sniffed you before I let you get this far," he added, the anger in his voice laced with self-recrimination.

"But if you touch one hair on her fine head, if you so much as sneeze in her direction, I promise you boy I will kill you with my own hands. I will kill you.

"Understand?"

"Yes," I answered.

"I will kill you," he repeated, pushing the doors open.

Inside the heat from burning stage lights hit me like a wall.

Navigating past the petrified black boards and monolithic stage props, the old man lead me to a vantage point where I could watch. Peering out behind a set of molted curtains, I could see only the back of Jasmine Brown's head.

"Everyone here tonight knows who I am," she said.

"I'm not Jasmine Brown, an educated, forthright woman of color."

"I'm not Jasmine Brown, daughter of celebrated activist and community leader Caisson Brown," she said as the audience murmured.

"I'm not Jasmine Brown at all," she repeated. "Who am I?"

Her arms rose, a full head of fine dark hair spread across her shoulders.

"The enemy of the deputy major, that's all I am," she shouted, her voice dropping into a deep recessive bass as the crowd rose to their feet in waves.

"The thorn in his side, I believe," she said.

"Because how we define a black person in our fine city," she said. "Is by who hates us, and he does."

The crowd roared, applauding, chanting her name again.

"But I am here to send a message to our deputy major" she said.

"To erase any doubts in his mind."

Dropping her arms, Brown grabbed the podium with both hands.

"That his discrimination, intimidation, and RECRIMINATION will not stand!" She said throwing her head back as the crowd erupted into a chorus of ear piercing screams.

"Not here."
"Not now."
"Not ever."

The auditorium writhed with lust and approval, ecstatic consent and electric fear. The crowd, pounding the floor, arms flailing with kinetic energy, teetered on the brink of chaos.

But Brown backed off the podium, waving her arms up and down.

The gesture restored calm. Suddenly it was quiet, within a minute, it was silent.

With the room eerily still, Brown bowed her head, mounting the dais again.

"Where are our dreams?" Brown said, rolling her neck so her face tilted skywards. "Who stole our dreams?"

"Our dreams are sacred, spiritual. Our dreams belong to us only. Our dreams belong to us Mr. Deputy Major," she said.

"The dreams of our people, the strength of our psyches, the marrow of our collective soul," she said.

"Our dreams are different from yours, Mr. Deputy Major."

Dropping her head to her chest, Brown slowly craned her neck, speaking the words slowly, dropping her voice on each syllable.

'OUR DREAMS ARE REAL!!!!"

The crowd exploded again, unleashing a tidal wave of approval that sucked the air out of the room.

And then without warning, I felt two hands on my back, pushing me from my perch behind the curtain. Off balance, I tried to grab a rope dangling from the ceiling, but the hands continued to push me forward until I tumbled onto the stage.

Lying flat on my back a yard from Jasmine Brown's feet, I raised my head just enough to see the old man pointing at me.

"He's a spy," the old man said. "He's a spy from the bureau," he screamed as the crowd fell silent.

I could hear Brown's footsteps, clear, loud, and precise.

As the crowd waited silently, Brown looked down, her left eyebrow curved in a curious semi-circle.

"Are you really from the bureau?"
"Yes," I answered.
"Don't move," she said, before returning to the podium.

"Security," she said as I lay on the floor, eyes fixed on the ceiling.

"Kill the cockroach," someone yelled from the back of the auditorium. "Kill the fucking cockroach."

"Kill him," screeched a thin, high pitched feminine voice.

And with that, the dam broke. A chorus of voices expressed the same. Not in unison, but broken and fragmented demands yelled from every corner of the room.

"He's got no right to live, none at all. Kill him. Kill him."

Brown stepped back from the podium. Paralyzed with fear, I lay still.

As the voices calling for my death seemed to collect into a single resounding demand, Brown stood serene, inexplicably calm.

Even as the audience surged towards the stage, eyes wet with rage, Brown was unflinching. Finally, as the old man grabbed me by the shoulders and started dragging me towards the waiting mob, Brown snatched the microphone from the podium and spoke.

"Enough!" she said, the force of her voice emitting a shockwave through the dusty speakers that hung from the ceiling of the auditorium.

"Let him go," she demanded as the old man released my legs.

For a minute Brown simply stared at me, her lips pursed, her pupils spinning.

"While I find it hard to believe that the bureau would be stupid enough to send this man to spy on us," she said as her lip curled upwards, a finger pointed at me.

“I find it even harder to believe that we would be so ignorant as to believe that killing this man, whoever he is, would do us any good,” she said.

“I can tell you, as I’ve watched my people suffer at the hands of the bureau, and in particular, watched our men disappear, I have dreamed that I could take a man like this apart, limb by limb until he bled for every sin his so-called organization has perpetrated on my people.”

”I can’t tell you how many times I have wished that I could crush the windpipe of the deputy major with the strength and power of my two hands, empowered by the rage of my ancestors,” she said as the crowd surged forward, all eyes on her.

“I can’t tell you how in my darkest moment, when the bureau raids our neighborhoods and takes our people away in vans that I wish I could raise an army to kill everyone of those jump-suited thugs right where they stand.”

“But I tell you now, we cannot do it. Not because I am peaceful by nature, or afraid to use violence to make my point, but for a far simpler reason:

OUR DREAMS ARE REAL!!!!!”

Uneven applause, outbreaks of tepid approval greeted her words.

“Our dreams are real, people!” she repeated, thrusting her arms over her head.

‘OUR DREAMS ARE REAL!” she shouted as she tilted her head backwards, her arms outstretched towards the ceiling. The applause now came in bursts.

O-U-R D-R-E-A-M-S A-R-E R-E-A-L P-E-O-P-L-E-!

As the crowd erupted, several men dressed in suits encircled me. A heavy set man, thick necked, wearing a black mock turtle neck and herringbone jacket grabbed the back of my collar, hoisting me to my feet.

Backstage, two equally large men grabbed me by both arms. Dragged through the empty halls of the school, I was carried out the door and tossed in the back of van.

It sounded like a mosquito – loose molecules that tickled my ear filling the air with an odd but sentient noise.

I raised my head, searching for the source. Engulfed in darkness, I could see only faint shadows, dark patches, traces of indistinguishable shapes.

I was lying in a bed, a thin blanket knotted around my ankles. My tongue was dry and swollen. My head throbbed.

Groping the wall, I searched for a light switch.

"I'm sorry," said someone I could not see.

"Christian?"
"I didn't think the record would wake you."

He cast a large fuzzy shadow a few feet from the bed.

I heard the click of plastic parts, followed by an electromagnetic pulse.

"The right type of music usually helps me sleep," he said. "And it seemed to work for you too."

"Where am I?" I asked.

He chuckled softly. "Now how I am supposed to know that?"

The low rumblings of bass guitar filled the room, followed by the soft hiccups of syncopated percussion. Then light strings, stabbing and aggressive. Finally the voice of woman, sultry, vague and haunting.

"Ever heard this one?" Christian asked.
"No," I answered.

The bass wobbled, the strings sagged, and the woman's voice descended into off-beat musings, a feline whisper. The drums would halt, and then resume, stripped down to a single sound, a smattering of bone dry congas.

The bass rode up the scale, bumping into higher notes until it dominated the upper register. A saxophone jumped in plumbing low frequencies vacated by the bass.

"What is it?" I asked.
"How should I know? It's your dream," Christian answered.

I laid my head down on to the cold mattress.

Occasionally an instrument would launch into a solo. The dry bass slapped against the walls. A kinetic saxophone hiccupped like a child. The woman sauntered through dark, colic phrases, drunk and unaware.

"Chaos funk," said Christian, now laughing as the song ended, the needle again filling the air with sub-atomic chatter.

"What the hell does that mean?" I answered, laughing to myself as I closed my eyes.

Only to be awoken again by the scratching of the turntable and smoke.

The door was cracked open an inch casting light across the cot. An old phonograph player sitting on a table next to the cot purred.

I could hear the sound of voices, including the unmistakable gravelly alto of Jasmine Brown.

I walked to the door, peering out through a sliver of space afforded by a rusty hinge.

The room was oblong shaped. A dozen floor lamps glowed brown and incandescent. Paisley tapestries hung from the ceiling, refracting light that blanketed the room with kaleidoscopic patterns.

Silver ashtrays mounted on pedestals formed obtuse roman columns. Large posters declaring rallies, concerts and lost poets, dotted the room.

At the end of a long table sat Brown, reclined in a high back swivel chair, the men who had carried me off the stage sitting, studiously watching her.

For the first time I could actually see her face. Her skin was light, caramel colored. A sharp nose offset by radiant brown eyes. Her eyebrows collectively long and thin. Hair, tousled, culled at the shoulders. She was simply beautiful.

"You're a crappy spy, Mr. Bureau," Brown said.

I opened the door.

"You need to work on your game."

"Where am I?" I asked.
"The only place that would have you, I would imagine," Brown answered as her followers turned their attention towards me.
"Why am I here?" I asked. "You could have dumped me in an alley."

Brown smiled, flicking a long ash off her cigarette.

"True," Brown said.

"That was our first thought, to dump you in the Claret River, or hog tie you and leave you in a dumpster to be discovered by rats, cockroaches, and the bureau, in ascending order of Godliness," she said.

"But then something remarkable happened this morning. I picked up the tablet, the Daily Star and what do I see on the front page but a story about you."

Grabbing the tablet, Brown stood the paper on its side.

"Reading about your impressive misdeeds," she snapped, "gave me the idea you might actually be of use."

She slid the newspaper across the table.

RECORDER OF WAIVERS UNDER INVESTIGATION

Source: Key official in District 4 accused of falsifying dream reports and taking bribes.

By Sylvia Shunt

A high level official working for Balaise's Bureau of Dreams is currently under investigation for falsifying dream reports and taking bribes.

Sources close to the investigation told THE STARLIGHT that the recorder of waivers in district 4, sector 3 is the now the focus of an expanding investigation into a scheme to grant phony waivers in exchange for money.

The unnamed employee has been missing for three days, authorities said.

Bureau officials declined to comment on the investigation, but the deputy major expressed confidence in the bureau's Internal Affairs Division after conferring with the council in a closed door meeting.

"We are working closely with investigation division, and both I and the council will continue to monitor the situation as the investigation progresses."

The allegations surfaced after the employee failed to report to work for several days, raising suspicions among bureau personnel that the employee was part of an alleged scheme to grant fraudulent waivers. A subsequent investigation uncovered several irregularities in multiple waivers requests, including a person who dreamed about death but was not remanded to the Waking Recidivist Complex.

The investigation has prompted an agency wide audit of waiver requests, a process bureau officials said could take up to six months.

Meanwhile, the bureau would not reveal the identity of the employee under investigation.

"Until we have more information ourselves and have detained the employee for questioning, we can't reveal any further details about the case," said bureau spokesman Thad Arlowe.

"However, we believe this employee should not reflect on the work of the thousands of brave men and women who put their lives on the line for the citizens of the bureau everyday," he said.

I dropped the paper. Brown and her cohorts simply stared at me. It was like reading about a dream, reviewing a waiver. The words added up to something to be judged, analyzed, and then digested.

But this time the synopsis ceased to resonate. It could not be decoded. This wasn't someone else's misery or someone else's dream.

This was about me. And it was false.

"Lies," I said.
"It's all lies, all of it."

Brown rolled her eyes.

"But everything they write about blacks is true, about how we don't cooperate, don't report our dreams," she said, taking a cigarette out of a gold case and placing it between her lips.

"It's hard for me to believe," said Brown, "that you would sit there and read that stupid article and the first thing you think about is that it's not true. Are you really that dumb?"

"I've worked at the bureau for five years," I answered, glancing at Brown's henchmen, who all watched me intently. "I've never told a lie."

Standing up, Brown circumnavigated the table, waving the hem of her silk skirt over a pair of muscular calves.

"You've worked at the bureau for five years?"
"Yes," I answered. "And the city for ten years."

Brown's eyes narrowed.

"What kind of career is it, to subjugate blacks, to ruin lives, to marginalize a people? What kind of career is that?" she asked.

"I never did anything wrong," I answered. "I never intentionally singled out a black person, not once."

"Then why were you spying on me?" she asked.

I picked up the article, thrusting it at Brown's face.

"Obviously I'm no longer a spy."

Brown raised her hand, gesturing towards her cohorts.

"But you were," she said. "Explain that!"

Brown struck a match. With a deft twist of her wrist, she produced a stick of incense. Lit, the scent of sandalwood filled the room.

"Explain," she repeated. "You have nothing to lose."

A week ago I would have used bureau speak, the indecipherable jargon embedded in the brains of waiver technicians to explain why I was indeed, a spy. I would have divulged one or two of our time tested methods for fixing bad dreams to satiate their curiosity, and then blamed my assignment on a procedural error, a lapse in judgment, or a bureaucratic snafu.

But now, with nothing to lose, not even a job, I decided to tell them everything. Every last detail.

So I told them the whole story. The truth as I understood it.

I told them about 9287, Sylvia, Reel and the bureau's secrecy. I told them about the increase in waivers, my meeting with internal affairs, the dream initiatives, and my mission: to get information on Jasmine.

They listened intently, all eyes fixed on me. They seemed excited, happy, nodding their heads with each revelation as if I was confirming a long held article of faith.

"That's it," I said.

Brown smiled.

"Maybe you're not a liar, Mr. Bureau, just terminally misinformed," Brown said.

"And now that you've told this story, a story that I believe to be true, you have indeed given me an option other than stuffing you in a Dumpster."

"I guess you could say you need a job," she said, laughing.

"But for now, go back to your room," she snapped.
"You're tired. You just don't know it," she replied.

Brown circled back around the table and sat down.

Folding her arms over her chest, she watched me as I slowly retreated, backing though the door.

I lay down on the cot. The sounds of Jasmine's voice drifted into the room. The discussion sounded heated in bursts as multiple voices rose into a jumbled chorus followed by eerie stretches of silence.

I examined the ceiling. An insect with dozens of legs, perhaps a millipede, sauntered along the far side of the wall. Legs flailing, its exoskeleton moved in perfect coordination. The bug seemed to glide, a frenzy of activity harnessed into a single forward thrust.

It was a blank room, just the turntable, a pile of magazines stacked against the wall, a threaded white throw rug and plastic lamp shade set on its side.

One thousand words. Maybe less. That's all it took - under a thousand incorruptible symbols to ruin my life.

The logic was lost on me, but the millipede was unstoppable. He paused at the crevice between the wall and the ceiling, half his body dangling across the void. Angling himself with unwieldy precision, he attached his limbs to the wall and scurried out of the room.

I scanned the walls for more insects. Fearless cockroaches that plagued my apartment or the wondrous spriggets, blackened grasshoppers with anvil shaped heads, nesting in the basement of district headquarters.

But the walls were spotless. Only the murmurs of Jasmine and her advisors, plumes of spiritual smoke and a faint scent of liquor plumbed the room with trace signs of life.

Closing my eyes, I pictured Sylvia climbing along the wall, her moonstone eyes attached to a porcelain shell, swirling like saucers. Her antennae fixed on the topography of invisible dents and depressions. Mirror eyes, one hundred translucent lids, blinking in cascades as she slithered between the walls.

It was a dreamlike imagining, definitely worth reporting to my dream counselor. I would have to remember it for my next session.

I was awoken by Jasmine.

"Wake up, Mr. Bureau," she said in whisper.

She looked fit in a pair of tight tan slacks with a white long sleeved shirt tied at the waist.

"You have work to do. Now get up."

Moving proved difficult. The thin mattress had left me sore.

"My father would say you move slowly for a relatively young man," she said as I struggled to get out of bed.

"Ms. Brown," I replied walking haltingly behind her. "I'd like to take a shower. And I don't think I've eaten anything for a day or two."

"Right here," she pointed to plate of scrambled eggs sitting on the conference table.

"You can shower later," she said. "Now eat."

Sitting down, I ate as Brown watched.

"I don't want to ruin your breakfast, but it looks like they covered part two of your sorry life."

I stopped chewing. Brown pushed the tablet across the table.

Investigation Widens to Bureau Employee

By Sylvia Shunt

The investigation of the alleged scheme to alter dream reports for money expanded today, after a supervisor of an implicated employee was charged with dream fraud.

Herman Reel, a 20-year employee of the bureau and the adjutant of District 3, Sector 4, is alleged to have taken part in the plan that prevented errant dreamers from being remanded to the bureau's Waking Recidivist Complex.

"Today due to the excellent work of the bureau's internal investigators we have uncovered a scheme that not only defrauded the citizens of the city of Balaise of money, but also threatened their safety," said the deputy major at a press conference on Tuesday. "Despite this unlawful act, the work of the bureau to move this city forward continues."

As part of the investigation, deputy major has ordered a full audit of District 3 dream statistics.

Meanwhile, the search continues for the recorder of waivers who is alleged to have hatched the plot that has raised doubts in the minds of many community leaders of the bureau's ability...

The eggs suddenly ceased to be interesting. I had lost my appetite.

"Everything happens for a reason, Mr. Bureau," said Brown, standing up.

"I could live without the nickname," I replied.

"You need to be reminded of your debt to my people," she snapped.

"I'll be back in an hour. The shower's around the corner. I put some clothes on your cot."

At the door, Brown turned and extended her arms.

“Stop feeling sorry for yourself. This is the best goddamn day of your life. You just don’t know it yet.”

“The best fucking goddamn day you might ever have,” she said, laughing as she disappeared behind the door.

I showered, found the clothes (a white button-down collared shirt and a pair of plain khaki pants), and took a seat in the ante-room.

The lingering stench of cigarettes and incense was overpowering. But the small alcove windows that dotted the room could not be opened. Thick red plastic sheets nailed to the frames made them impenetrable eaves.

A poster on the wall caught my eye. It was Brown perhaps ten years younger, her hair longer, braided.

TO APPEAR TONIGHT – AT MILT HEAVEN’S LOUNGE

ACCLAIMED JAZZ SINGER – JASMINE BROWN

Her white teeth dazzling set against dark skin glowed, her smile as wide as the poster itself. Strands of fine dark hair splayed like a cosmic cloud about her face.

Suddenly Brown burst into the room.

“Move it, Mr. Bureau,” she said.

A large bookcase in the corner of the basement was pushed partially to the side by Brown’s body guards. Behind it, a door. Outside, I was led up a staircase. A beige van idled at the top of the stairs, parked backwards at the end of a long claustrophobic alley.

"Get in," Brown said, gesturing towards the back.

"Better not to be seen," she said as motioned for me to sit next to her.

"I come and go, but nobody knows."
"What about the bureau?" I asked.
"They haven't found this yet, and for now, I think they'll stay away," she added. "Unless they come looking for you."

The door shut, the engine started, and the van moved with a velocity that knocked me off the seat. The vehicle changed directions and altered speeds so violently I was alternately pinned against the window or pressed into Brown' unforgiving shoulder.

After several minutes, the van jerked into reverse, and suddenly stopped. The back doors opened automatically.

"Follow me," said Brown, leading me into an alley, then down a musty stairwell.

We entered what looked like a large storage room. Light bulbs dangled from the ceiling like electric eyeballs. Rows of gray file cabinets stood like grave markers.

A table with a single reading light sat in the clearing, walled-in by an endless hedgerow of file cabinets.

"Have a seat," Browns said, closing the door behind her.
"Just us," I said, noticing the sudden absence of her bodyguards.
"Yes, just us," she said.

Adjusting the lamp, Brown placed her cigarette in the ashtray. She dropped a legal pad and pen on the table.

"We know the bureau is looking for you. They've even hit a few of our regular spots," she said. "It's only a matter of time before they find you. At this point, it's a race against time."

"I don't understand," I replied.

Brown inhaled, spreading her fingers across the top of the table.

"If they find you, we both know you'll never see the light of day. They'll lock you in the complex until you cease to exist."
"They can't do that," I argued. "Not unless a certified dream counselor..."
"Shut up," Brown yelled, standing quickly, her chair tumbling onto the floor.
"Haven't you been paying attention?" she stammered. "My men wanted to stuff you in bag and leave you on the corner.... I said no, he can be useful."
"But talking to you now," she said, shaking her fists, "I think I made a mistake."

Brown plucked another cigarette from her silver case and lit it.

"The truth is, strike back, or you're history."

Brown stood up, opened a file cabinet drawer, and pulled out a file folder. Without even bothering to open it, she flung its contents across the table, scattering paper like leaves.

"What are the four primary dream categories, Mr. Bureau?"

The question caught me off guard. "I don't understand?"
"Typologies," Brown said. "Name the typologies," she repeated.

"There are many typologies of dreams, multiple geneses, and of course four primary categories, at least on the negative side."

"Name them, the primary categories," she said, circling the table.

"About death, about violence, about theft, about rape," I recounted.

Brown smelled of vanilla and rose.

"Tell me what that dream report says."

Sorting through the papers strewn across the table, I found the box that listed the primary dream diagnosis.

While the subject has manifested elements of many types of dangerous dreams, lack of cooperation and unsubstantiated claims of innocence make it difficult, if not impossible, to rule on the status of the most predominate dream archetype at this time. Therefore the patient will be classified as "indeterminate," and remanded to custody of the bureau until further diagnoses can be made.

"I've never heard of indeterminate," I said, turning to look at Brown. "Never."

Brown opened a drawer and pulled another file.

"Same diagnosis on this one," she said. "In fact, the whole drawer is filled with so-called indeterminate dreamers," she said, lifting an entire file drawer of folders and dropping it on the table.

"I don't understand. We've never used that in my sector," I replied. "They're gone, all of them," she said.
"What do you mean gone?"
"Remanded, then indeterminate, and then gone," she said.

Disappearing behind another row of file cabinets, I could hear Brown opening drawers.

"Gone, gone, and gone," she said as she reappeared with more files.

"No one is supposed to be remanded without a specific diagnosis," I said. "With this type of report, a person could end up in the complex..."

"Permanently," Brown replied before sitting down.

"Permanently and perhaps forever," she added.

Slowly, Brown pushed the next stack of folders as high as pile of morning waivers across the table. Dust, dirt and residual mold floated into the air.

"How many?" I asked.

Light revealed circles under Brown's eyes, golden half moon ruts sown into her skin.

"I don't know. I haven't counted, but let's just say enough."

I opened another file. The paper work was filled out to the letter of the law. The dreamer was male, black, and young, similar to the previous case Brown had shown me.

The case used almost exactly the same diagnostic narrative as the first: "A patient was detained by the bureau during a sweep of areas designated as a 'hot spot' by bureau dream analysts. During intake, the patient WAS diagnosed with a 'disposition to dream negatively.' Based on the diagnosis, the patient is to be transported to the Waking Recidivist Complex for further evaluation."

At the complex, after a series of dream counseling sessions, the final diagnosis was always the same.

"The patient's poor state of mind is the cause of his psychological instability, making him unfit and unsafe to be returned to the civic population. However, due to lack of cooperation on behalf of the patient, his dream diagnosis is indeterminate and he shall be remanded until such time as a more definitive diagnosis is made."

I looked at another file, and then another. Twenty cases later a pattern became clear. A black male diagnosed as indeterminate and then remanded indefinitely.

All were signed by the same person, the Chief Examiner of Dreams, Dr. Adi Schuler.

"How did you get these?" I asked Brown.
"We have sources inside," she answered. "Deep inside," she added.
"Now start taking notes," she snapped.
"Why?" I asked.
"Because," Brown said leaning over the table, grabbing the collar of my shirt.

"You're going to find our men."

I never questioned her orders.

I didn't necessarily sympathize with Brown's ordeal. I wasn't really concerned about the fate of black men.

I was like many bureau employees, skeptical of the blacks. Bad dreams put blacks in remand, not the bureau.

But Brown's dilemma provided me an unexpected opportunity.

I had never heard of a Dr Adi Schuler. But unlike the mysterious dream No. 9287, my lack of knowledge meant it was possible Schuler's "indeterminate" diagnosis was as unknown to me as it was to bureau command.

If Dr. Schuler had indeed created an unauthorized dreaming typology, then I had a more enticing secret to offer the Deputy Major than a few scurrilous details on Brown's love life. IID would no doubt be interested in an unauthorized dream diagnosis. Turning in Dr. Schuler at the very least would take the heat off me, and possibly provide me with a bit of leverage to negotiate my return to duty.

Still, Brown didn't give me much time to reflect.

For several weeks I was awoken by a zephyr of cigarette smoke dangling above my face, courtesy of Brown. Everyday I was treated to the same meal of watery scrambled eggs and burnt white toast, and then transported to the basement to perform my research.

My days were spent mostly alone among the files, no breaks, no lunch. Dozens of files, thick folders of mimeographed dream reports lifted from the bureau's archives.

"Whoever got you these files could probably find the men faster than me," I said to Brown one evening as she sat in her chair smoking a pencil thin cigar.

"Never use your pinky to do a job worthy of your thumb," she replied before gulping down a shot of brandy from a snifter.

As I pored over reams of paperwork and dream reports, the advice of my trainer at the Dream Academy, Dr. Fran, remerged.

"There are the science of dreams typology and the art of dream typology," he said, standing on a small step ladder he used to bolster his five foot frame.

"We must practice the art of dream science,"

At the time the significance of his advice was unclear. Meaningless clichés, an odd turn of phrase made dream science mysteriously exciting. We were preparing to "recondition the soul," he would often remind us.

"A dream about death may have no tomorrows," he spouted in the middle of in class exam. "But can it be stopped today!"

And now, poring over dozens of reports, the art of dream science seemed more relevant than ever. In a style born out the mastery of the metaphor, and a narrative made compelling by simple repetition, the bureau had managed to deposit hundreds of black men into the equivalent of a dreamer's no man's land.

"The dreamer was witnessed by bureau personnel loitering in an area designated by bureau analysts as high risk area for bad dreaming... When asked what the dreamer was doing in the area he was uncooperative with bureau personnel.

...approached by bureau personnel the suspected dreamer fled...

Why run, why flee from us?

The dreamer declined to answer questions, or refused to move on when ordered by bureau personnel, or declined to discuss his last five dreams when asked. The dreamer was uncooperative with bureau personnel... The dreamer had been detained five times by bureau personnel for not reporting dreams.

Dreamer observed in the company of bad dreamers.
Dreamer evidenced negative behavior.
Dreamer was uncooperative.
Dreamer has previous record of bad dreaming.
Dreamer used foul language and was abusive to bureau personnel.
Dreamer failed to obey a lawful order by bureau enforcement agent."

It boiled down to one large case of non-compliance against a single race: devious, well constructed and obviously effective.

"I never realized the bureau was so good," I said to Brown.

"You must be fucking kidding me," she snapped.

As the days passed, I reviewed hundreds, then thousands of cases. My notebook filled with names, ages and dates of remand, all carefully documented.

But despite working as fast as I could, Brown became more and more impatient.

"We can't hide you forever," she said one afternoon as I worked.

Often I was left alone with only a small jug of water and a box of plain table crackers.

But occasionally Brown would sit with me, chain smoking while I read through file after file.

"You need to work faster," Brown ordered as I added names to my list.

"The bureau's looking for you," she said.

"Work fast."

Along with the pressure from Brown, the daily articles recounting my alleged misdeeds continued unabated.

I had led a secret life, according to Sylvia Shunt.

Her articles revealed how I pocketed proceeds from my scheme to trade favorable waiver reports for money, and then blew the cash luring sex hoarders into the bowels of Balaise's most decadent hovels.

Soaked in liquor, I plied the alleys of Balaise, preying on desperate dreamers, offering them a route to salvation for the price of a drink.

Later, lost in a labyrinth of debts unpaid and addictions unsated, I framed my conscientious supervisor, using his seal to certify false dream reports.

"We are all relieved that this terrible chapter in the bureau's proud history is over," the deputy major was quoted.

After the fifth or the tenth story, the feeling of nausea that coiled in my stomach every time an article appeared began to fade, replaced by detached curiosity. It was, oddly enough, like witnessing my own dream, living in an alternate reality, on the border of what is true and often not blended like a cheap hovel cocktail.

At night, if Brown was not scheduled to speak, she would lounge in the main room of the "Den" as her body guards called it, the subterranean facility where I lived.

The Den was a labyrinth of small, sparsely furnished bedrooms, compact bathrooms, a large kitchen and a spacious storage room filled with food, liquor, cigarettes.

Accessible only from an alley, the entire complex of rooms sat below an abandoned building, hidden away like an interminable basement.

After I had completed my daily work and we had all eaten, Brown and her bodyguards would pour brandy into paper cups to drink, smoke and listen to records while I served as their impromptu DJ.

"Put the record on, Bureau Boy, the one with the red label," Brown barked.

Brown's vinyl collection was stowed in the corner of the Den's lounge. Several dusty stacks of obscure soul records, remnants of Balaise's vibrant funk movement. Rummaging through the offerings and randomly selecting a disc became a nightly ritual.

As the music filled the room, Brown and her people would tilt their heads back in unison, drawing a collective breath exhaled on the downbeat. The first few bars of a new record would halt conversation, silencing us all. Then Brown would drop her head, clap her hands, screeching.

"Now that's soul, isn't it?"

Heads nodded in agreement.

"Real soon, right Bureau Boy!"

I too would nod my head.

Nightly, I would repeat this routine watching as Brown and her cohorts got drunker, the music got louder. By midnight, the rafters would shake as an oblong cloud of cigarette smoke drifted over heads.

"You know Bureau Boy," said Brown one evening when she was particularly drunk.

"They think they're going to find you," she said, sipping her drink.

"They think they're getting close, but they won't, and do you know why?"
"No," I answered.

Brown rose from her chair, sauntering towards my post at the turntable, her wide hips suddenly unwieldy and plastic.

"Because we're gong to turn you into a black man," she said to a chorus of jeers.

"Can you believe it?" Brown said, dragging the back of her hand across my right shoulder.

"Does it scare you?" she asked.
"No," I answered.

Placing both her hands around the back of her head, I could smell natural oils, vanilla and rose, musk and earth. Her finger nails dug into my skull.

"Does it scare you?" She repeated.
"Not as much as it does you," I answered.

Brown smiled, shaking my head from side to side like a can of paint.

"We're going to make you a black man," she laughed, stroking my hair.

"You're going to be our stealth bomb."

That night, when Christian visited me, I knew I was dreaming.

The air was thick, hard to breath. My mouth sterilized by thirst, my lips numb and immobile.

In the darkness I could sense him, his presence coiled in the corner, all energy and invisible matter.

"I'm not awake," I said as soon as I spotted his form gathering like a funnel cloud.

He chuckled.

"That's your business; I'm not the one dreaming."

Blinded by a watery darkness, I could barely distinguish the outline of his body against the blank, lightless wall.

"It's too dark, I can't see you," I said.
"I know," he replied.

There was no music in this dream, just an odd buzzing sound, the unruly trills of static electricity.

"What's that's sound?" I asked.
"I think it's the sound of night, the sound of the dead night," Christian answered.
"I don't understand."
"Neither do I," he said, as the buzzing grew louder.

Even in the darkness, I could see noise, the tiny elastic particles bubbling in dark soup, churning like a billion mites feasting on blood.

The moist electricity ran in visible currents, streaking in cascades of static heat before fading into a blazing trail of dimming electrons.

"It's like we're in some sort of soup," I said to Christian."The art of electricity," he replied.

Christian moved, his arms unfolded, his head nodding from left to right.

"Are you ready to die?" he finally asked.
"No, I am not," I answered.

The buzzing was now coming in bursts. Christian's shadow dissembled, scattering into fractals.

"I'm not ready to die," I replied.
"I understand," he answered. "But tomorrow you leave."

Presently his form began to shift from side to side, pulsating like a quantum ghost.

"I almost can't hear you."
"This is it," Christian said, his form rising, unraveling, and seeping towards the ceiling.

"This is the sound of your death," he exclaimed as my eyes grew hot, sparked by electrons thrown into orbital disarray.

"The sound of your demise."

Christian, or his remains, became indistinguishable from the dark. The buzzing sound became jagged; a sudden burst of light stung my eyes.

"This is finally it," he said.

I was awoken before dawn. Two bodyguards marched me into the storage room. Brown was waiting.

Without speaking, she led me into a bathroom, turned on a light, and handed me my ID.

It had been altered. My name was now B.R. Smyth.

Brown grabbed my the arm, thrusting me in front of the mirror.

"Look," she ordered.

The mirror was set crooked, cracked, covered with dust, and blotched with paint. The bathroom was poorly lit, shadowed and musty.

My unshaved beard was ragged. Dark wormy circles swallowed my eyes. I was skinnier too.

Brown produced a baseball cap and placed it on top my head.

"You will go to the recidivist complex," she said. "And find our men."

"They'll nail me in a second," I answered.

"Really," Brown replied.
"Look," she snapped.

Small tufts of ragged hair bled out the sides of the baseball cap. My skin was mottled.

"I look tired," I said.

Brown leaned over my shoulder, her soft hair brushing against the back of my neck.

"What do you see?' she asked.
"Me," I replied.

Brown grimaced, angling her cigarette towards the light bulb.

"You still see the bureau employee, the honest hardworking man. The productive citizen of Balaise who worked tirelessly to incarcerate my people."

"But if you look closer, you can see the criminal now," she said, stroking my shoulder.

"You can see the man who defrauded errant dreamers, the man who bribed his boss to cover up crimes," she continued.

"Believe in it, and you slip by like a shadow," she said.

We studied my reflection. My face hadn't changed, but my eyes looked dim, my lips peaked.

"They'll just think you're a junky."

Brown grabbed the top of my forehead, placed her lips on my cheek and kissed me.

"Now go," she said.

The van parked on the corner of Mount Avenue. A business card for the All Good Catering Service was placed in my hand.

"Call this number when you find the men," Brown said as I exited the van.

It had been weeks since I had seen the light of day. The air was crisp, cool, but still soaked with carbon and diesel fuel.

Balaise was alive, its morbid sense of sameness intact, dull sunlight made duller by the gray skin of sullen row homes.

Moribund trucks, tail-pipes hot with carbon tailed five dollar cabbers. The sidewalks remained fiercely uneven. The shadows of rats flitted against walls of calcified brick.

Walking towards a bus stop, I noticed a group of people huddled near the corner. As I approached, a line of bureau agents were assembled along the sidewalk.

"One at a time," a bureau agent dressed in full battle regalia barked.
"This is plain harassment," said a stocky, broad shouldered black man wearing coveralls.

"Nothing short of harassment," he repeated.

The agent grabbed the protestor by his collar.

"Detain him," barked an officer. "Charge him with disorderly conduct."

As I neared the lineup, I felt an odd semblance of fear. In my normal guise, I would slip past this line, unencumbered and unnoticed. But now it seemed unlikely.

"Hello Mr. Junky," said a thick, muscular officer with a porcine face.

"Get in the fucking line or we'll detain you too," he yelled.

I stepped into the line.

"ID," the bureau agent asked as he ran a nightstick over my body.

"Any weapons?" he asked. "Tell me now and we'll go easy on you."
"No sir," I answered, handing him the doctored ID.

The agent stared at it for a moment,
"You work for us," he asked skeptically.

"Sarge, take a look at this," he said as he handed my ID to his superior.

My stomach knotted. The agent passed my ID to the sergeant.

"Call it in, it could be fake," he ordered without looking at me.

The agent pulled a communicator from his gun belt.

"I work for the bureau," I said to the agent.
"Shut-up," he replied.

"Dispatch over," said the agent, who continued to stare at the ID.
"Over," said a female voice,"
"I have..."

Suddenly a blood curdling scream spread panic along the line. People began scrambling in all directions.

Like a herd, the bus riders formed a wedge headed towards the street, a wild scrum of panicked pedestrians that nearly knocked the sergeant on his ass.

"Get your hands off me, get your hands off me," screamed a woman I could not see.

The sergeant was tossed against a utility pole, twisted like a pretzel as he brandished a black stanchion.

With brute agility, he dove into the crowd, swinging his club, extricating bodies with fierce, withering strokes.

Watching his hands, I saw my ID fall to the ground trampled under a melee of combat boots and sneakers.

I scrambled to retrieve it, but a sharp kick in the head sent my body rolling back onto the edge of the sidewalk.

I crawled along the asphalt, my head aching. For a second my ID disappeared under the boot of a bureau guard. But as he hoisted a heavy set woman with a wild mane of gray hair to her knees, his boot lifted.

I rose to my haunches and tunneled forward. Scooping the ID into my hand, I curled into a fetal position, waiting for the commotion to end.

Within minutes, as panic spread along the boulevard, the guards dispersed, leaving me and a few other unlucky pedestrians lying on the sidewalk. I scanned the street.

Bureau guards were scampering down alleys, squads spread out along Mount Avenue. The sound of sirens grew quick on the horizon. An old woman lay on her side, her glassy-eyed stare wise and unsettling.

I rose to my knees, navigating past an overturned trash can. Safely concealed behind the bus stop, I peered out, looking for bureau agents.

A block down Mount Avenue, at least half a dozen agents in full riot gear were busy erecting a barricade. I wouldn't make it past another check point; I had to run, and run fast.

An alley across Mount Avenue looked like a safe bet. A small crevice wedged between two grimy, half collapsed structures.

I waited, watching the guards drag saw horses out of the back of a bureau van

A bureau commander with gold epaulets appeared. The guards quickly assembled in a line as he surveyed the hastily erected checkpoint.

I ran.

Motivated by fear, my legs felt lighter, disjointed. I sprinted across the boulevard, past two lanes, the embankment, tripping as I went airborne off the second curb.

On the third lane, I heard the voice.

"Stop."

But I didn't. There was only one lane left to cross. I was twenty feet from the safe embrace of a serpentine alley.

I could hear several sets of boots grind into the pavement, righting overweight bodies in my direction.

I ran faster.

But just inches from the makeshift hovel, my head was suddenly thrown forward, a searing pain burned the back of my neck and froze my legs in mid stride.

My elbows blunted the fall. Through blurred vision, I saw a night stick spin like a boomerang, coming to rest against a curb.

Immobile, wracked with a throbbing pain and skin deep asphalt burns, I could hear the drumbeat of heels getting closer. I lifted my head just slightly, quickly thrusting my knees beneath my chest. Like a sprinter, I coiled my ankles beneath my body.

"Slow down Junky!" a guard yelled.

I sprang from a crouch position and hurtled into the alley. I scurried like an animal, fast and frantic, into the blackest hole I could find.

In no less than a second I was two blocks deep into the dark, hollow crevice of piled bricks and mildewed mortar.

I could hear the boots, heels skidding, slipping and sliding, batons scraping brick, grunts and expletives. But I was too far into the dead neural pathways of Balaise to be found.

Burrowing into the steep side of a hollowed-out row home that branched into a maze of nondescript rooms, I flattened my body on the ground as they yelled threats, splayed flash lights, and shot flares.

But this was my labyrinth now. Intruders were not welcome.

Balaise's alleys were indeed arterial. One could wander for hours, turning corners, crossing in back streets, moving miles without encountering a major boulevard or a person.

It was forgotten territory, a wasteland of wreckage and dust. Piles of crumbling brick and petrified mortar accumulated several feet deep. Septic vines kneaded pavement into unwieldy lumps, hidden obstacles difficult to navigate.

Eyeless abandoned buildings shed scraps of copper tubing while metal shavings glistening with the golden hue of autumn leaves.

As I passed an empty row home, its windows worn into large holes, a fetid breeze stopped me in my tracks.

I could see a television standing on its side. A purple couch flipped upside down, springs protruding, varicose veins bloodied and sequin. Magazine covers, stained with residue of rain.

A cloud of mosquitoes hovered over the mass of pocket books, ankle boots, tennis shoes, soda cans, and empty cigarette packs.

Gum wrappers piled onto the remains of phone bills, dunning letters, surrounding a blackened baseball sutured with yellowed Band-aid, and the web like strands of a black wig, spider legs, plastic veins pasted to a thin layer of mold.

The stench of rotted flesh fouled the alley, an odor that filled the air like a thick coat of grimy paint.

I moved on.

The small glimpses of sunlight, errant rays that managed to escape Balaise's ceiling of gray guided me. Regardless of how the alleys twisted, turned, disappeared, and sometimes shriveled to a space that forced me to shimmy sideways – I always headed South.

I shared the caverns with rats and cockroaches, squirrels and stray cats, but not people. Silent and shrouded from traffic, the alleys formed an urban cloister.

Every few hours I would find a comfortable perch on a pile of bricks and eat a piece of the cheese Brown had placed in my jacket pocket.

And then as dusk cast an orange glow on the underbelly of the cloud cover, I smelled it.

Downtown.

Blinded by the twisted fire escapes, rusted trash cans, and blackened windows, the scent of downtown Balaise was the first clue that the Waking Recidivist Complex was within reach.

It was a combination of odors – the smell of rotted garbage, the street vendors selling Balaisian sausage mixed with stench of diesel fuel – lofted into the air by steam leaking from treacherous pipes that flowed into antiquated heating conduits.

The aroma guided me. The putrid stench of the complex was in the air, all metal and flesh, perspiration and pneumatic tubing.

A few deft turns and I caught a glimpse of the complex's massive towers.

Standing in the alley, I could see its gleaming stanchions, its rising tide of foiled brick, fallow aluminum stretched over unwieldy curves and floating galleys.

It looked more impressive now, like a felled asteroid.

Stepping out of the alley into an unusually sunny day, I felt exposed. Walking on the sidewalk, my baseball cap twisted, a wiry beard flecked with dust, I was suddenly naked.

I headed towards a back entrance known only to bureau employees.

I entered through a revolving door. A security guard sat in a folding chair reading a tablet.

"ID," he said without looking up.

He glanced at it and nodded. I entered a concrete tube lined with portals.

The tube proceeded down a steep vertical incline. As I neared a wide, double door, I felt tactile energy, a stream of agitated molecules crawling up my skin.

Inside, I was stunned by the size of mechanical organs that powered the city's dream complex. Brass dinosaurs with arching tubes suctioned to the ceiling throbbed with steam. Ceramic centipedes, sprouting tubular umbilicals, twisted and tangled into a mass of muscular conduits pushing air into hundreds of miles of ventilation ducts.

A canopy of plastic hung over the trembling tops of rapid machinery. Thick boughs of cables rooted in the ceiling coiled over strands of pneumatic tubing twisted into synthetic branches.

Unsteady in the magnetic wake of a million reels of electric copper, I stumbled forward, swaying as I walked.

Past several of these massive machines, a wide, rectangular door appeared.

I opened it and entered a long hallway, steam billowing from pipes inches over my head.

At the end of the hall stood an elevator, and next to it, a plaque displaying an alphabetized list of offices. Dr. Adi Schuler's office was on the basement level.

Turning left, I proceeded down another hall so thick with cables it was nearly impassable. The hum of combustion machinery was replaced by the monotone buzz of electric circuits.

Turning the corner, a glass door appeared. Painted across the door in bold black letters:

Dr. Adi Schuler

Inside a plump old woman sat at a desk, her wide streaks of magenta blush blurred by the hot flash of fluorescent lights.

"Yes," she said.
"I'm here to see Dr. Schuler."
"You are?"

I produced my ID.

"Community relations."
"Regarding?"

Sitting in the lone folding chair, I shook my head.

"Just let him know I'm here."

The woman grimaced, stood up, and left the room. Several minutes later she returned, plump, well rounded, stitched into a dull gray skirt.

"He'll be with you shortly," she said.

A half hour passed before Dr. Schuler appeared, a tall lanky man with an angular mustache and an uneven beard.

"You wanted to see me?"
"Yes."
"Come in then," he said.

His office was a large but not spacious, inundated with over-stuffed book shelves, file cabinets, dusty file folders, magazines and tablets.

Plopping down behind a broad mahogany desk, Dr. Schuler picked up a journal and started to read.

"Excuse me, Doctor."
"Yes," he replied without taking his eyes of the journal.
"I have a few questions."
"Go ahead," he answered.

Unsheathing my notebook, I turned to a blank sheet of paper.

"I work in community relations, district nine," I said.

"There have been complaints about large numbers of dreamers who essentially disappear in my sector."
"Yes," the doctor replied, his swollen gray eyelids nearly closed.
"Family members who do not to know what happened to their loved ones."

The doctor opened his eyes.

"Isn't this an enforcement issue?"
"Perhaps," I replied.
"Then why are you telling me about it?"

The doctor returned to the pages of the journal. A silver cylindrical clock sitting on his desk ticked off seconds. The purr of active ventilation ducts rattled the floor.

I waited. He continued to read. Finally I asked.

"Doctor, are you aware of a dream typology called 'indeterminate'?"

He did not stir.

"'Indeterminate.' Are you aware of it?" I repeated.

"Doctor?"

Finally, he responded.

"Indeterminate," he repeated.
"Yes, indeterminate," I answered.

"Impossible."

Leaning over his desk, the doctor shuffled a stack of papers, glaring at me, his irises drowned in black.

"Sector Nine?" he asked.
"Yes," I answered.
"And what do you know about indeterminate?" he asked.
"Only what I've been told by families."
"Really," the doctor replied.
"One wonders how a community relation specialist would stumble upon something so arcane."

"A typology has not been cleared through a general dream order," he continued.

"Never taught at the academy."

"Unknown to the profession."

"And now today, a community relations specialist simply shows up in my office without an appointment – whom I've never seen before and claims to have first-hand knowledge of what may be a mystery even to me."

The doctor frowned, thrusting his hands under a pile of books. Seconds later, he unveiled a cigarette.

"So the question then becomes, who are you?"

I handed my ID across the desk.

"Smyth. Never heard of you," he said.

"I find it strange that a community relations specialist would be meddling in dream science."

"So I ask again: Who are you?"
"Who I am is not half as interesting as what you've been doing," I answered, thumbing through my notebook.

"I have here in my notes thousands of names, dreamers who have been ruled indeterminate and remanded," I said. "But the oddest thing is that all of these dreamers have something in common. Do you know what that is Doctor?"

"Enlighten me," he answered.
"Every single dreamer is black," I replied. "All of them, their dreams ruled indeterminate, are black."

The doctor stiffened. His eyes darted, his mind seemingly in the midst of a strenuous calculation.

"That doesn't strike me as interesting," the doctor replied. "Not interesting at all."
"What's more interesting is who you are," he added. "And I think I have an idea."

"What's more interesting actually, is how interesting a story in the tablet about a program that locks away black men in the Waking Recidivist Complex indefinitely," I snapped.

He tossed his cigarette into an empty soda can.

"Don't be a fool. What makes you think the tablets are interested in blacks?"

"Just a hunch," I replied.
"Well I can tell you they are not," he said.
"Can't say for sure," I replied.
"I can tell you this, too, the indeterminate program has made this city safer." he said pointing at me.

"We've made the city safer for blacks, and for everyone else," he added.
"They don't agree," I replied.

The doctor exhaled.

"They," he responded. "How would you know?"

I tapped my book.

"Because I have all their names, and they, as you said, are not happy."

"That's not news," the doctor replied. "The blacks complain no matter what we do."

"Take Jasmine Brown's neighborhood. We've improved quality of life there dramatically," he continued.

"Less crime, less drug use, less negativity in general."

"And yet all she does is complain," he said.

He paused, shuffling papers.

"So, are you a reporter?
"No," I replied. "But I'm curious. How do you fit thousands of men in the complex? Where do you put them?" I asked.
"The men are not held in the complex," he answered.
"But where then?"

The doctor opened a drawer beneath his desk. He pulled out a pack of cigarettes.

"Are you a reporter?" he asked again.
"No," I repeated.

The doctor eyed me as he lit the cigarette. Pausing to inhale, he leaned forward.

"It's a miracle really," he whispered. "Something that has worked out beyond my most optimistic hopes."

"A plan that has transformed the bureau," he added.

"When the bureau first began its work, the whole idea of dream science seemed at best ineffective. Yes dream intakes were high, remands were high, everything was working as it should," he said, exhaling.

"But the changes in the neighborhood that we expected were not occurring."

"About violence, about death, all on the rise."

"Economic development stalled, new projects delayed."

"And so I was asked to come up with a more aggressive plan," he said, stubbing out the cigarette.

"I was asked to make the bureau work and save the city."

Bending over his chair, the doctor retrieved a glass. Reaching under his desk, he unveiled a bottle of whisky. Tilting the bottle sideways, the doctor poured a drink, lifted it above his head, and downed the contents with a swift flick of the wrist.

"So I came up with a plan , a simple plan," he said, refilling the glass before raising it to his lips.

"And it has worked."

"You mean indefinite remand?" I asked.
"Indeed," he answered.

Pouring another drink, the doctor continued.

"The plan, as I saw it, was to use a blanket diagnosis, a diagnosis that fixed all the holes in the deputy major's dream theory."

"We need to do more than remove the negative thinking from the black community, as the deputy major planned," he went on.

"But the bad element as well," he continued.

"And we couldn't be bothered with all the paperwork and ambiguity of a simple dream diagnosis," he said.

"The blacks were not suffering from a problem of the mind, but a disease of the soul," the doctor said, a vein along his temple fidgeting like an inchworm.

"The indeterminate program was the answer, the best way to remove the bad actors, the bad thoughts," the doctor finished.

"So the deputy major approved?" I asked.

"Not at first," the doctor said, downing his second drink in a single shot.

"At first, in fact, he didn't know," he said. "But as the program progressed and our success became evident, we presented it to the deputy major who gave his blessing for the bureau to apply it citywide."

"And now, every sector in the city with a majority black population has an indeterminate directive."

He paused, studying his glass.

"And then there was 9287," the doctor sighed. "The dream within a dream."

"When it appeared in Brown's sector, we knew we had a problem."
"Why?" I asked. "What was the dream?"

The doctor closed his eyes, lowering his head until it touched the side of his desk. After a minute of silence, he exhaled.

"Do you want to see?" he asked.
"See what?
"How it works," he said, continuing. "How the indeterminate program has helped save this city."

"You want to show me?"
"A work of art must be seen to be appreciated," the doctor replied before pouring himself another drink.

The engine of the doctor's bureau vehicle purred as we bounded up Founder's Boulevard. A steely dusk turned phosphorous, dropping green splotches of tattered light on the hood. The doctor's deep set eyes and spackled hair looked suddenly like seaweed.

As the car moved along Founders Boulevard, we sat in silence. The mid-afternoon rush buried the streets in pedestrians. Cabs with bulbous tops and sequined doors darted in and out of traffic.

"Have you ever considered what might have happened to Balaise if we did not open the bureau?" he asked.

"Have you ever thought what we might have done if we had never developed dream science?"

"Not anymore," I answered.

The transmission stalled, and the car lurched backwards. The doctor pounded the brake with his foot, and the engine roared, sending the car forward with a burst of torque.

"It's something you should consider," he said. "Given your situation."

The car entered Founder's Circle. Spinning the steering wheel like a turntable, the car veered to right, then entered the access road to Turner's Point.

"The Brownfields?" I asked.
"Exactly."

Turners Point, or the Brownfields as it was known, was the abandoned site of the city's industrial past.

A swath of land bordered by the ancient harbor, the Point was a beachhead of skeletal remains, rusted hulking leftovers – a reminder of the sinew and sweat that produced the bulk of Balaise's wealth.

A set of twisted metal gates marked the entrance. As the car raced onto a cratered boulevard, street signs bent like dead trees.

Husks of empty factories stood like giant Sheffields. Rusted rib cages stripped of brick sprouted from the earth. Tall islands of grass, halcyon weeds, swallowed wobbly spires of brick.

Abandoned coke ovens stood like hollow mausoleums. Pockmarked smoke stacks trembled, bent towards the ground, throwing up bricks like tubers.

The deputy major called the Brownfields a "gem by the water." He often stumped for redevelopment. But decades of industrial waste soaked into the ground like a permanent second skin made the entire patch of real estate toxic .

Still, I would have never imagined the bureau would find use for it.

Suddenly the car jerked to the left, launching us down an unpaved road. A few hundred yards later it came to a stop just as the city's first - and I thought abandoned - prison emerged from the wrought-iron jungle.

It was a castle, with turrets, sandstone crenellate and large wood doors. Two guard towers blotted out the sun.

Set back against the green waters of the harbor, it looked like a medieval palace, severe, imposing.

As I exited the car, the doctor stood by the driver's side door, head thrown back, eyes now black stones shining in the mid-afternoon haze.

"Follow me," he said.

"Normally remanded dreamers go to complex for treatment," he said as he led me towards the gate.

"But these cases were so complicated, and fraught with peril that it was decided the patients required special care," he explained.

The doctor knocked on the door. A small portal opened. He placed his ID on the glass.

Seconds later, the door swung open. As we entered, a heavy odor of unwashed flesh and burnt institutional meat filled the air. The hallways gleamed with the afterglow of an industrial strength cleansing. Voices echoed in the halls.

The doctor motioned for me to follow as he turned a corner and ducked into an office.

Inside I was suddenly surrounded by a wall of blinking screens. Hundreds of video monitors were stacked to the ceiling, thousands of incandescent view panels sparkling with images.

Wading through thick piles of cables and splitters on the floor, I stood next to the doctor as his head swiveled, surveying the images with avid agility.

The images changed, flitted, and sank into pools of septic gray. Everywhere I turned, the silhouettes of what appeared to be men, moving, marching, grooming, sitting in chairs, watching attentively, bloomed and then faded .

The monitors were numbered, collated with colored dots, thick pieces of tape cordoning them off into quadrangles.

"It's amazing," the doctor remarked.
"How many....," I said, stopping.
"I don't know. I've never counted," he answered.

"As you can see," he said while he watched, "from this room we can monitor all four sections of the complex."

Pointing toward a bank of monitors divided by a thick black line, the doctor continued.

"Each dreamer spends part of his week in a different section where he undergoes therapies designed to address the four primary categories of negative dreaming."

Moving closer to the bank of monitors, I studied a screen.
"I don't see anything?"

He pointed at a monitor in the corner.

"Right now we have a group of men who are undergoing immersion therapy for about violence," he said.

"And here," he said, the tone of his voice rising, "we have another group of men undergoing what we call awakening for about death."

I squinted at the screen, trying to decipher their movements. The darkness of their skin, the poor lighting, blended their faces into a stream of static.

"I really can't see."
"Here," the doctor said, pointing at one of the screens.

The screen flickered for an instant before filling with white light, and then went blank again.

The doctor tapped the bottom of the monitor with his forefinger. Suddenly the faces of men, blotted out by hovering black squares reappeared.

"Look," he said.

I could see a raised hand as the camera panned back and forth.

Body parts flowing across the screen disembodied – flowering for a moment, then evaporating.

"I don't see it."

The doctor waved his hand across the monitor.

"There, there, look!" he shouted.

I saw faces, black faces, smooth and inelastic. The doctor pointed to a different screen.

"What you're seeing are the results of the bureau's best work," he said.

"We are reclaiming their minds, and they are now dreaming of better days," he said.

"Imagine what these men would be doing, left to own devices, living in Balaise," he said.

"They would be criminals, thieves, poor fathers, misguided and anti-social."

"But in here, they are anything but that," he continued.

"In here they learn a skill, a trade."

"They learn to cope with their anger."

"They even make things," he said, pointing to a monitor that was at the moment blank.

"What kind of things?" I asked.

"T-shirts, mugs, souvenirs for the tourists," he replied.

"Now that Balaise is safer, tourism is up," he said.

"And it is no accident that the opening of the Indeterminate Dreaming Center has coincided with the rise of economic activity across all sectors of the city," the doctor exclaimed.

"We have changed the course of Balaise simply by removing those who would not or could not contribute to its betterment," he explained, pointing at a screen that panned across a wide auditorium of faces.

Suddenly a screen blinked. A man was sitting in chair. His hands appeared locked at his sides.

"Is he handcuffed?" I asked.

"Only the least cooperative are restrained," the doctor said.

On another screen, the same image: A man restrained on what looked like a cot.

"You know that not all dreamers have the correct mindset," the doctor replied.

"One of the first steps of our indeterminate program is to help dreamers to learn how to control impulsivity," he added.

"If they can't, we use minimal restraint periods to correct behavioral issues."

"After which they are kept confined until they adjust."

"But as I was saying," the Doctor continued, waving his hands across a bank of monitors. "They learn a trade or skill, and along the way make things."

"All wages go to their care, and all proceeds pay for the program," the doctor added with a smile.

"It is what we call in the business a win, win, win-win-win, and then some," he said chuckling.

"And now that you've seen it, I feel better.

Much better."

The doctor turned and waved at a surveillance camera hanging from the ceiling.

From the corner of my eye, I spotted two bureau guards entering the room through a back door.

I looked at the doctor, averting my gaze from the approaching guards. He was smiling, whistling.

"So, are you ready to go?" the Doctor asked.
"Where?" I asked.

"To settle into your new home," the doctor replied, pointing a finger at the bank of monitors.
"Perhaps we can help you understand the true failings of Jasmine Brown," he continued. "The deputy major would deem her – because he is a bit of an intellectual stylist – a 'moral insurgent'," the Doctor said.

"But to me, she is more common, what we like to call them in Balaise, 'troublemakers.'"

The Doctor smiled as the bureau guards sidled up behind him.

"I've got a better idea," I offered.
"I'll walk out the door."

"Impossible," the doctor replied. "And almost as foolish as your failed plot to march into my office and expose the indeterminate program," he added.

"Foolish by design, Doctor," I replied.

"If I don't return to Balaise proper within 36 hours the thousands of names – all my research – will be handed over to the tablets."

"That's a pile of crap," the doctor laughed. "You really expect me to believe that you planned ahead with such skill that I am in jeopardy of being exposed for doing what? ...Making the city safer!!!!" he yelled. "Are you kidding?"

I took baby steps backwards towards the door as the doctor spoke.

"That a mindless bureaucrat turned criminal has hatched a plot that will destroy the indeterminate program – the most successful bureau enforcement tool yet," he said taking another step towards me, the bureau guards in tow.

"Oh if only the deputy major could be here to witness this."

I mimicked the doctor's movements, closing in on the exit, maintaining a measured distance between us and the doctor.

"Maybe he'll simply read about it," I countered. "And then I can only imagine what Jasmine Brown will say when the story is told of the bureau program that had thousands, perhaps tens of thousands of blacks remanded indefinitely in a toxic prison making souvenirs."

"I'm sure he will be pleased to wake up to that story," I added.

"The blacks, the blacks will thank us. They have thanked us for making their city safer. They'll celebrate once they know what we've done for them," the doctor argued.

"Perhaps when your so-called story hits the tablets, we can offer to send their men back. We can bus them all together and drop these thousands of men you seem to think are inexplicably innocent back into the neighborhoods. I'm sure the blacks will hold parades, celebrations, and welcome them all with open arms. Until they realize along with their men comes crime, degeneracy, violence and economic hardship. I can just imagine the joy that will spread throughout Balaise when there men are returned."

"Maybe they'll anoint Jasmine Brown, their self-proclaimed leader mayor. The mayor of black town – and then she and all her cohorts can do to the rest of Balaise what they've done to their own neighborhoods. Together, with all their men," the doctor continued, breathing rapidly, pupils dilated.

"They can rebuild the city, repair the dilapidated housing, reduce crime, create jobs, all of these things can be done by these men," he said pointing frantically at the blinking screens.

"But you know what? Nothing will happen. Jasmine Brown has done nothing but complain, nothing but create an industry of dissent. She can't even muster enough black votes to challenge the deputy major," he added.

I felt the cold steel door knob in my hand. The doctor smiled.

"Go," he said. "It's almost dark, if you survive the Brownfields – which will be tricky – then we'll pick you up in Balaise," the doctor said.

"And if you manage to cross the Brownfields unharmed, and I doubt you will, and then go to Balaise, bring your story to the tablets, and you'll discover the true meaning of disinterest," the doctor said.

"You think you're on the verge of something great don't you? Some sort of poetic justice to compensate for the fact that you were run out of the bureau. A little bit of revenge, exposing us all."

"But think twice. Think more than twice before you act upon your idiotic ideas," he offered.

"The problem is, if I remand you now, you'll simply spend the rest of your pathetic life in this interminable hole. Wasting away, rotting with your own delusions of grandeur. I would prefer to watch you stumble out that door into the great unknown, fail, and then spend the rest of your life wondering why."

"How sweet it will be when you, the recorder of waivers, discovers his bureaucratic skills are of little use on the streets of Balaise, in the most violent, corrosive city known to humanity.

Out there, amongst the animals, beyond the safety of the bureau walls. Nothing will give me greater pleasure than to witness your humble return and your permanent remand as a shell of the man that stands before me now."

"So go, go to the Brownfields. If you survive, we'll find you," he said, gesturing to the guards who quickly retreated.

"And think about it," the doctor added as I opened the door. "Can you save this city?"

I walked out of the prison, as the eyes, but not the bodies, of the bureau guards followed me.

As I walked past the gates, voices of indeterminate men floated into the molten air, evaporating into the ether of the Brownfields.

Devoid of street lights, disconnected from Balaise's electrical grid, the Brownfields were submerged in darkness unlike any other patch of municipal property in modern civilization. Only the evanescent lights of downtown, spread like a mist over the darkened industrial remains, provided a sense of direction.

Guided by those lights, I headed home.

The skeletal remains of factories that had gleamed in the haze of dusk were now reduced to towering shadows, blurred blackness lurching toward the sky.

A brisk wind bristled through ancient steel dream catchers, filling the air with hollow tones.

I stumbled on to the remains of a boulevard, a wide stretch of unencumbered dust surrounded by prone street lights, fallen like dead trees.

Rats scurried, kicking up loose chucks of gravel and calcified lumps of sod.

The moonlight glittered too off the backs of cockroaches, bleeding insect tracers etched in odd mounds of dirt.

Beside the wind, the Brownfields were solemn, a quiet graveyard. No pedestrians, gypsy cabs, diesel trucks, or joyful hovels. No wrought-iron diners, chicken and waffle shacks, or claustrophobic corner stores.

Walking along the cratered boulevard, I thought of the doctor.

Was he right, I wondered? Was Balaise better off without certain blacks? Without the troublemakers?

What if he was? What if the bureau was the last best hope of Balaise? What if Jasmine Brown was wrong?

Suddenly, a voice caught my attention, a half whisper that seeped out of the shadows.

"Over here...you, over here."

The whisper came from the husk of hollowed out gas station. I peered into the darkness, seeking its source.

"You, what the hell are you doing?" the voice whispered again.

"Get over here quick!"

"You don't have much time."

I spotted two hands, finger tips lit like quick sliver, curled into a fist, waving frantically.

"There isn't much time. Hurry."

I crouched low to the ground, approaching like a cockroach.

Climbing over a curb on my hands and knees, I spotted the fist, waving in the air out of a broken window.

"In here man, hurry,"

Crawling past a row of rusted out pumps; I scurried through a doorway.

Inside, a single candle cast caramel light on several bodies huddled in a corner.

"Fool" was the last word I heard before the back of my head was lit on fire.

Awoken by voices, I opened my eyes to blackness as thick as death.

Shadows flitted against a concrete wall. A fire burned in the distance, embers cast into the air like fire flies.

Several yards away a group of men talked in low whispers, their faces obscured by flames.

I pushed my body upright, bracing my back against the wall. Pain radiated from the back of my neck and down my vertebrae to the base of my spine.

Suddenly one of the men turned around.

"You're lucky to be alive, fool," he said, with an even, low frequency voice.

"Even I don't go out after dark."

"I didn't have much choice," I answered. "I was forced to walk back to Balaise."

The man chuckled.

"How did you get a hold of these?" he asked, thrusting my notebook towards the fire.

I quickly scrambled to my feet. Lunging towards his outstretched hand, I tried to grab the notebook. But like a bull in search of a matador's cape, I missed, it was withdrawn, sending me stumbling to the ground.

"Give it to me," I demanded.

For the first time I could see the speaker's face. His skin was dark velvet, his face long, framed by a large forehead silky smooth and bathed in sweat.

As he stared at me, a piece of silver glinted against the light of the fire. A knife dropped from his palm.

"You try that again, I'll cut you up like a turkey," he said, rotating the blade deftly with his fingers.

"You ain't nobody to me. Only reason you're breathing is so I can find out where you got all these names," the man said, thrusting the notebook towards me.

"I've been working this corner for more than two years. Ever since they re-opened that prison we've been taking down the drug mules, the stray women, and whoever else is fool enough to try and pass through," he continued.

"Most of the time we get a few dollars, a few rocks of dream soup, or piece of ass worthy of the time it take to drag it through that door," he said.

"But I've never seen anything like this, a notebook full of names, names I know for fact are stuck in that damn jail."

"Those are the men," I answered. "The men incarcerated in the prison by the bureau."

He stared at the notebook, turning it over in his hand while the men behind him murmured.

“You mean these are the men in the yard,” he said, pointing in the direction of the prison.

“Yes, those are all the men the city has incarcerated, part of the indeterminate program.”

“What do you mean ‘indeterminate’?” he snapped.

“It’s a dream diagnosis that the bureau has so far managed to keep secret.”

The man started flipping through the pages, his eyes electric, bloodshot, feverishly scanning columns.

“I know them, I know a lot of them,” he repeated.

After several minutes of reading, he closed the book, tossing it on the ground.

“I don’t know what the fuck you mean by ‘indeterminate,’” he said, the sweat on his brow mutating light emanating from the fire.

“I don’t know what the fuck you’re doing here, but I can tell you one thing, I know some of those cats,” the man said, his head swelling like a balloon.

“And lot these niggers belong in that goddamn jail, bureau or no bureau.”

“All the men are black, all from the poorest neighborhoods,” I replied.

The man laughed, softly at first, then a gut wrenching belly laugh.

“What kind of fool have I dug up,” he said, turning towards the now light-hearted black chorus bobbing their heads with approv-al.

"I drag you in here figuring you couldn't be too bright, given that you're crossing the Brownfields in the middle of the night with nothing but a notebook."

"But now I'm here talking to you about some bureau bullshit while you're telling me the reason you have this list. Is it because you think these niggers should be where – back on the street?"

"I didn't say they should be out on the street," I replied. "I was simply asked by Jasmine Brown to find out why so many black men had disappeared from the Balaise."

The man shook his head, sending a cloud of spittle into my face.

"Jasmine Brown, now she's a piece of work. She ain't done nothing for black folks except get her name in the paper and cause all sort of trouble."

"But what you don't understand is that the people on that list belong where they are. Men that have done black folks more harm than good. Niggers that can't hold a job, can't pay their bills, all around no good."

"What you've put together there is collection of the most useless, no-good niggers the city of Balaise has ever produced," he continued.

"And I'll prove it," he said.

"This here page has the name of my cousin Henry Jamison," he said. "Let's see if it burns."

With a quick thrust, he ripped a page out of the notebook, tossing it into the fire.

"I don't know what you're real game is, but if you think you're doing blacks any favors by helping Jasmine Brown shaking down white people with one of her schemes, you're as good as a thief to me."

"I ain't but one man trying to make a living, but I can tell you this much, it's not the bureau that fills that jail, it's the world of niggers," he said, flipping through pages of the notebook.

"Here's another name, a no-good nigger I knew from the West side, he name is Melvin Blunt."

"Let's see if he burns too," the man said, ripping a page out of the notebook, crumbling it into the ball, and tossing it into the fire.

"Nothing but flames," he said as the choir laughed again.

"Whatever bullshit Jasmine Brown put into your head, I can remove with my fist," he said, clenching his hands.

"And just what did you think you're going to do with these names? You gonna walk up to the jail with a notebook and say 'Free Them Thieves. Free them perverts. Free them nigggers!'"

"Was that your plan?" he asked, the chorus again erupting into laughter.

"I didn't really have a plan," I answered. "Once I found the men, I guess I would have brought this to the tablets," I added.

"Good thing I caught you," he said, "before you went and did something stupid," he said, tossing the notebook on the ground.

"After I finish eating I'll burn the rest."

The night air had turned stagnant, black, unflinching and stifling.

The muddied walls of the abandoned gas station bottled the heat like a coffin.

I was an idiot. Lured into a trap, now sitting on a dirt floor in the middle of the Brownfields waiting for what, to be executed?

Most troubling, was my captor's hatred of Brown. I understood the doctor's malice. Who could blame him? But Brown, hated by blacks too?

Welcome to no-man's land, I thought.

Suddenly one of the men spoke up.

"Boss, Boss, look!"

One by one the members of the group – at least five in all – crawled under a nearby glassless portal.

They whispered to each other, occasionally standing up, before sliding back down onto the floor and crouching against the wall.

Torches were lit. Water was tossed on the flames, engulfing the room in a cloud of fly ash.

Plotting in a small huddle now gathered under a window, the leader relayed orders in sharp, brittle whispers.

"He just dropped a package no... Gotta be a mule...straight from the prison. He should be heavy with loot."

While they plotted, I set my sights on the notebook.

I crawled towards the fire, ignored as the men frantically planned their attack.

"You," the leader yelled. "Don't move."

"I want the notebook," I yelled without thinking.

"Shut the fuck up and keep down," he said, brandishing the knife.

"You two," he said pointing a pair of men huddled next to the fire. "Get out there and flush him out."

"Get out behind, chase 'em down and we'll get him."

Two lanky men stood up, quickly scampering out the back door.

"I'm taking the note book and I'm leaving," I repeated.

"I told you once I would carve you up," the leader threatened. "Now go sit your ass down."

Without thinking, I stepped forward, crouching next to the notebook.

"I work for the bureau," I said. "And I bet they don't know about your little pirate's den."

"But I'm sure it would take just a few bureau agents to clean up this mess and deposit you and your friends in prison."

In a split second the leader was on top of me, his cold hard hands wrapped around my neck, the quick silver knife pinched against my throat.

"I told you I'd cut you," he whispered.

Suddenly a cry pierced the stagnant night air. The leader pushed me to the ground and scrambled back to window.

"Fucking niggers got friends," he exclaimed. "It's on."

In a split second the leader leapt out the portal, two associates in tow.

Left by myself, I sat stunned for a minute, listening to guttural shrieks and manic cries of pain that followed.

I heard feet scuffling, a series of grunts followed by a hollow scream.

Clutching the notebook, I quickly rifled through the pages, checking to see if my collection of names was still intact.

Suddenly a red blotch appeared on the cover, a small circle of what looked like blood.

And then another.

And then the droplets of blood fell like rain. Droplets that grew wider as they filled the page.

I placed my hand over my throat. Hot liquid flowed between my fingers.

Quickly I thumbed through the note book, searching for a blank page.

But before I could finish, the sound of voices echoed through the room. The pirates were returning. Without thinking I tore out a page, slapping it against the cut.

I snuck out the side door, crouching under the shallow rays of moon light as I ran past the disemboweled gas pumps and out into the Brownfields again.

For hours I stumbled around with little sense of direction.

The landscape had turned lunar. Chunks of ancient concrete, surly rocks and castaway iron bars bruised my feet.

The bleeding had stopped. The notebook paper stuck to my neck like a second skin. Dizzy, I wandered aimlessly, hoping to leave the Brownfields, or at least find a decent spot to sit.

The beacons of downtown had vanished. The prison was unseen, buried in a blanket of oil soaked mist. Only the whispers of the wind, the faint unsettling of rust stirred beneath the cover of nightfall accompanied me.

I walked over ancient rock, crusty shells of industrial mollusks. Pig iron shrapnel tore at my feet. Jagged shards of fractal steel and colored glass gathered into a foul nest of predatory steel brambles.

Each step produced new pain. In the glint of the shallow moonlight I could see the tattered remains of my bureau pants splattered with blood.

I entered what appeared to be a widening street. A boulevard maybe, bounded by large gaping square frames set several yards apart. Ancient eyelids, fossilized and worn.

The widening road divided into two halves, separate lanes surrounding an unseen mass, a compost of anti-matter.

At the fork, large iron spikes emerged in the darkness. Stepping toward them, I was confronted by a tall, sinewy fence. Behind the fence loomed a shapeless mass of nothing.

Standing in the street, I stared, waiting for my eyes to adjust to darkness. The wind bristled now. A faint cry echoed.

A pair of wild eyes suddenly appeared. Set apart by a long cylindrical shaft, I realized I was staring up the nostrils of a horse.

The horse's hoofs dangled in the air. Perched atop the animal sat a steel-jawed man wearing a tricorne hat, a long coat, and furrowed sleeves.

A series of quick shouts caught my attention. Strong, staccato yelps that sounded successively closer.

But I was transfixed by the beast, the dark rider, the statue now abandoned, a grave marker in an abandoned grave yard.

Another round of shouts prompted me to clench my fists. The horse still dangled in the air, hooves lit by fire. The dark rider's face seemed to ventilate light. A dim pair of eyes burning like torches.

But the last shout whacked me behind the ears, so I ran.

Stumbling down the street, the smooth road gave way to uneven path of angry bricks.

Splayed like tubers, every step pushed me off-balance, my feet slipping and sliding.

The visceral screams suddenly seemed closer, faint warnings sounding from the darkness.

But the unsettled road slowed me down. My foot caught a pile of bricks, throwing my weight forward. I tumbled to the ground.

Pain radiated in waves from the bottom of my heels to the back of my head. My joints stiffened, legs tingled, stung by glass tentacles and concrete knives.

Slowly I stood up, untangling my arms as my joints congealed into knotted clay.

Fearing my limbs would suddenly freeze, I broke into a forced walk, this time taking long uneasy strides, planting my feet firmly before each step.

I was tired, hungry, and disoriented.

The moonless night had given way to odd purple darkness, an off-color seamless dream.

The voices continued to sound closer. Monoliths and husks blanketed by darkness ceased to be interesting. My only thought was downtown.

Heavy limbed, my tongue dry. The curtain of darkness grew into tendrils of blanketed lines and geometric shapes.

In the bowels of this dream, the darkness ran over my body like a cool, indelicate stream of water.

A star rose from the muck, unblinking, redirecting my gaze.

Walking with my neck craned towards the sky, my battered feet now stopped moving altogether.

The night sky pried itself open revealing a bowl of stars, a bottomless pit of shine.

In the glow of the Milky Way, I resumed walking. The stars grew brighter, malignant. I saw clusters of atoms, globular light bulbs that burned the tip of my nose and knocked me off balance.

The light came crashing down like hard rain, a radiant glow soothing my joints.

The stones turned on their backs. The path grew smooth and inelastic. The cockroaches retreated, burrowing underneath the toxic dirt. The bullying shadows melted into murky lumps of clay.

What were these stars I had not seen? The lights of the city hid them, but now I saw for the first time the candle of the universe burning inside of night.

A brightness that defied the light bulbs caked with dust rot stuck beneath a tide of dirty lamp shades in hundreds of Balaisain apartments. Or the broken night light in my bedroom, or the pulsating neon bulb that hangs over my desk.

None of those lights could match the brightness of the stars.

And so I walked, faster, ably, the voices, threats, unheard. I glided across the Brownfields like an angel, unsullied by dirt. My fingernails clean, pain reduced to a lingering thought, someone else's muse. Jasmine was laughing, calling my name, her light cryptic voice echoing in my head.

I ran, my thighs churning with anger, my arms suddenly unwieldy, pain throbbing in my forehead gave way to a full throated roar. It was a lion's roar - a fearless unholy roar that summoned the clear and silent moon, lighting the Brownfields gray sullen glow with a magnificent noise.

I roared and ran and ran until I could run no more.

I was awoken by a sharp prick in the back my neck.

"Mister."

Eyes opened, I stretched my back until my head was upright. Chain links of metal fence dislodged from my skin.

I turned around. An endless fence formed a steel barrier between the Brownfields and the rest of Balaise.

"Mister," I heard again. Standing next to the fence was a young boy dressed in a tiny black overcoat and corduroy pants.

"Mister," he said again, his brown beret crooked and bent.
"Yes," I answered.
"The hole is over there," he said, pointing.

I walked several yards. At a juncture where the fence turned slightly, east, a sizable hole stretched from one side to the other.

Dropping to my knees, I crawled on my haunches retracting my head like a turtle until I was lying on the sidewalk.

It was an unusually sunny day. Bright unprocessed sunlight bathed otherwise malted sidewalks. Mortared towers dissected with running faults looked painted against a backdrop of sunshine and tangled rays.

Invigorated by my midnight run, I took a deep breath, exhaling slowly.

Suddenly I remembered the notebook.

Dislodging it from the seams of my pants, I thumbed through it, unleashing a heavy cloud of dust. The majority of the names were still legible - only a few obscured by blood stains.

Stuffing it under my arm, I now had to decide what to do.

The doctor had given me slim odds to make it across the Brownfields. It was possible my kidnappers were employed by him.

But even if he believed I would fail, it seemed unlikely that he would leave anything to chance, including the possiblity that I would remain free long enough to expose him. I had to assume he would hedge his bets, put out a city wide bureau notice – a 24/7 remand order, giving me little time to complete my task.

The story of a secret indeterminate program had to be told. It was my best chance to escape permanent remand.

The tale would be simple: I'm a whistleblower, not a thief, crucified by the bureau for trying to expose a program that unfairly targeted blacks.

But rather than heed my concerns, the bureau tried to destroy me.

So instead of a corrupt employee who took bribes to support a drug habit, I would be hero unjustly smeared because I tried to stop program that was victimizing the blacks.

Not a bad plan.

I headed towards the best last chance to tell my version of events: the Daily Star's competitor, the Balaisian Weekly.

The Balaisian was a long walk from the Brownfields. The paper's offices were situated far across town in a neighborhood of abandoned warehouses and collapsing sheds known as the Old Storage District.

Once a thriving distribution center for the city's port, the streets of the Old Storage District bore the angry scars of neglect, miles of abandoned train tracks, wasted arteries, varicose veins, sullen and muted sunk into the ground.

The rusted rails spread like an exoskeleton through back streets and side alleys – twisted tines slithering below hovel doors.

'The district" – as it was known – was a vast warehouse for the finished goods manufactured by the citizens of Balaise. But as the city's industrial base decayed, the neighborhood ceased to be of any real use.

Now it was an arts district, with large barn size hovels, vintage clothing stores, and empty long houses packed with withering used books.

It took an hour of traversing heavily trafficked downtown boulevards before I arrived at the Balaisian offices.

Set back against a narrow canal, the paper's headquarters seemed oddly bent, warped by age.

A façade sagged like a dim black eye. A neon sign sketched in bright plastic pink proclaimed THE BALSIASIAN across the door, scripted in a stylized neo-cursive.

Entering, I found myself standing in a large, undivided room. The cavernous ceilings, buttressed by thick Maplewood arches, were dotted with low-slung fans that twisted softly, stirring the smoke-filled air like an ancient stew.

A young man with manicured sideburns and ring affixed to the side of his nose sat in a chair, reading a book.

I stood near the door for several minutes, hoping he would notice me. But he remained immersed in the novel, barely breathing as I waited awkwardly, clutching my notebook.

Finally I spoke.

"Excuse me."

The young man looked up, his plain face unnaturally white, offset by corpse-like eyelids, bathed in an ultraviolet wax.

"What's up man?"
"I need to see a reporter."
"Yea, you have an appointment?"
"No?"

I fumbled through my notebook before ripping out a page, dangling it in the air like a talisman.

"I have information about a secret bureau program that I would like to share," I said. "A secret program that no one knows of."

"You're not crazy, right?"
"No," I answered.

He picked up a phone, dropping his head behind a svelte, modular desk. After conferring for a minute, he hung up.

"Alan Shevron will be with you in a moment."

Satisfied, I entered the spacious bullpen.

The maze of prefabricated walls was disorienting. The clicking of keyboards, the soft undertone of hushed voices in staccato conversations conjured the presence of an unseen hive.

"Can I help you?"

I turned around. A tall, thin man with slicked back hair and a broad nose stood next to a cubicle. His mouse-like eyes looked unnaturally feral. He was bundled in a tweed jacket and a steel-colored shirt open at the neck.

"Yes," I answered. "I have something I think you need to see."
"Well come in then," he replied.

I followed him inside the cubicle. Shevron sat down at his desk, pointing to a chair set alongside a wall. Extracting a notepad from a drawer, he thumbed through several pages while I waited.

His cubicle was littered with paper, stacks of documents bound with twine, file folders stacked on top of thick embossed reports.

"So what do you got?" he asked, eyes fixed on his notepad.
"A story about a secret bureau program," I answered.
"Really," he said, his paper-thin voice rising as he scribbled.
"A secret program?"
"Yes," I replied. "The bureau has been running a program called 'indeterminate' which removes black men from the streets and keeps them housed in the old city jail indefinitely."
"I have here a fairly complete list of the names of all the men," I continued. "And I've seen it myself."

Shevron slouched forward, lowering his head over the top of the notebook, writing furiously.

"Let me see," he said, without looking up from the pad.

Taking the notebook out of my pants, I pushed it across his desk.

Turning on a rectangular table lamp, Shevron quickly scanned several pages before setting the note book aside.

"Where did you get these names?" he asked.
"Jasmine Brown."
"Really," he said "Jasmine Brown?"
"Yes," I answered.
"And so you claim the bureau is running a secret program that takes black men off the streets illegally?"
"It's not a claim. I've seen it myself," I replied. "They're housed at the old prison in the Brownfields."

Shevron continued to take notes, his eyes firmly glued on his notepad.

"Do you mind if I copy a few pages?" he asked.

"No," I answered.

Stuffing the notebook under his spindly arm, Shevron bounced out of his chair and exited the cubicle.

I waited.

Yellowed clippings, articles with his name written in bold imposing fonts stretched across the cover of several tablets pinned to the walls of his cubicle.

DREAM BUREAU SUCCESS: RECLAIMS LOST NEIGHBORHOOD

DREAM ENFORCEMENT CALLED ANSWER FOR FAILING CITY

DEPUTY MAJOR ANSWERS HIS ATTACKERS

And then finally

THE REAL JASMINE BROWN: TROUBLEMAKER'S HIDDEN AGENDA IN BATTLE WITH THE BUREAU

As I scanned the headlines, it occurred to me that I may be sitting in the wrong cubicle.

Just as I decided leave his office, he returned, my notebook in hand.

Sitting down at his desk, Shevron rubbed his eyes with clenched fists.

"You think this is good enough," he said, thrusting my notebook across his desk.

"You think this is good enough evidence to write a story questioning the effectiveness of the dream programs?" he asked, the tone of his voice rising with each syllable.

"I've been there. I saw the men. I saw it for myself," I replied.

"Maybe," said Shevron before turning in his chair to face me. "But do you know how this program has affected the neighborhoods? Do you know if crime has gone down? Has quality of life improved?"

"No," I answered, pausing. "I don't."

"You see, that's not good enough," said Shevron, flashing an uneven smile.

"Have you studied, for example, the real estate values in the neighborhoods affected by this indeterminate program?" he continued. "The real estate values?"

"Have you?" he added with a high pitched, near yelp.

"No, I only know that the men are held indefinitely, and that bureau has kept the program secret," I said.

"The only secret is how successful the bureau has been," he snapped.

"But you," he continued, "have decided that success is not good enough."

"Obviously you have not done your homework," Shevron said, pointing at my notebook.

"I have almost every name of every man in the program. I visited the prison with Dr. Schuler, the creator of the program, and I have seen it all for myself."

"That's not good enough," answered Shevron.
"Why?" I asked.
"It' just not good enough!" Shevron replied, his lip curled beneath his nose. "IT'S NOT GOOD ENOUGH !"

"It's not good enough to expose a program, just because you've seen a few men receiving treatment, or talked to a few people predisposed to dislike it. That's not good enough, at least not for a journalist!" Shevron said.

"What if the program has improved the neighborhood? What if has reduced crime?" he asked.

"And what if Jasmine Brown is lying?"
"Why would she lie?"

Shevron opened a drawer, extracting a huger file folder sutured by several thick rubber bands.

"Did you know that Jasmine Brown defaulted on a mortgage?" Shevron said, tapping the folder. "Did you know her brother has failed to pay child support?"

"Did you know," Shevron said, quickly removing the rubber bands from the file, flipping it open and spreading papers on his desk.

"Did you know she has been taken to court six times for unpaid debts?" he added.

"And...her driver's license was suspended for six months after she failed to renew it on time!" he said, quivering in his chair, panting with excitement.

"I didn't know, but I don't see your point. What does Brown's court record have to do with the men?"

Shevron bowed his head.

"It has to do with the credibility of Brown," he said.

"It has to do with her motives."

"She didn't put the men in jail," I replied.

Shevron blanched as he shuffled through the fluttering stacks of papers now spread across his desk.

"That's why you're not a journalist, and I am," he answered gruffly.

"And Brown isn't the only one with credibility problems," Shevron added.

"It's not like I don't know who you are."

I shifted uneasily in my chair.

"Am I supposed to believe that story of an ex-bureau employee under investigation for selling waivers?" he asked, turning to face me.

"I am supposed to believe you," he said, offering a wave of spittle accentuated by a gap between two protruding large front teeth.

"I am supposed to believe that you're telling me the truth."

"Everything they wrote about me was a lie," I replied. "I didn't do anything wrong."

"Well then why the investigations, why the stories in the Starlight? Are you calling Sylvia Shunt a liar?" he said, clenching his fists.

"No, it was the bureau that made up those stories," I answered. "They lied about me because I told Shunt blacks received worse treatment by the bureau than whites."

"Oh, oh, please," Shevron replied, belching after each incantation of "Oh." "You expect me to believe that you are an innocent, oppressed whistle blower? Are you serious?"

"I don't care what you believe, but I'm telling the truth about the bureau."

"Did you come to this conclusion before or after you lived with Brown?" He asked. "Is that when you decided to become a civil rights hero?"

"Brown pointed me in the right direction, but if I hadn't seen it for myself, I wouldn't be here," I replied.

Balling a piece of paper in his hands, Shevron paused. Turning his chair clockwise toward the back of his cubicle, he wiped his nose with the paper ball before spinning the chair completely around to face me.

"You're a lair!" he shouted. "You're in league with Jasmine Brown. You're a crook, run out of the bureau, and now you're trying to use the press to spread lies."

Grabbing my notebook off the desk, and holding it in front of his face, Shevron stood up.

"This isn't good enough. Do you understand? It isn't good enough!!!"
"No, I don't understand," I answered. "I saw it for myself."

"That's not good enough!"

"The men were locked in prison, with no procedure for their release."

"That's not good enough," he repeated.

"And all the men are black," I added.

Shevron quickly scooped up a pile of papers, shuddering as he launched an unstable pile into the air.

"THAT'S NOT GOOD ENOUGH!" he yelled, covering his ears.

"It's not good enough," he repeated, settling into his chair.

His desk phone rang.

"Yes," he said. "Okay, send them in."

"The good thing is," he said, plucking papers off the floor and dumping them onto his desk.

"Is that we know who you are."

"So," I answered. "That doesn't matter to me."

Shevron smirked, a broken crescent.

"It matters to them," he said, pointing over my shoulder.

I could smell them before I turned around: Bureau guards.

As recorder of waivers, I was last best hope for an errant dreamer, the final appeal before internment at the Waking Recidivist Complex.

Therefore as I rode silently in the bureau van, I laughed as I wondered if I still had the right of waiver.

"Can I file a waiver request?" I asked the two ground-beef bookends sitting on either side of me.

But the expressionless brutes did not reply.

The van pulled in front of wide metal gate. Two massive doors slowly disappeared. I noticed the word INTAKE written in bold letters across a blackened portal.

Once inside the gates, we stopped at a thick yellow line extending from the door of a small office across the tarmac. The guards exited the van, grabbing me by the scruff of my neck, practically tossing me onto the tarmac.

"Stand here," the guards said.

A tall man with a fallow goatee approached, his stomach protruding like a balloon beneath a red sweater vest. Drumming on a clipboard with a pen, he circled me for almost minute, sizing me up like a head of cattle.

"We finally found you," he said. "The infamous recorder or waivers who defrauded the bureau."

"And now you are going to experience remand first hand!" he said.

"I can't wait," I answered.

Remand was more unpleasant than I imagined.

For two hours I stood in a long serpentine line that barely seemed to move.

Then I was fingerprinted, strip searched, and probed in the ass. Shoved into a small white room by a female guard, I was photographed and ordered to don a brown jump suit with my remand ID number emblazoned across the back.

Finally I was stuffed into a claustrophobic cell with no place to sit, standing shoulder to shoulder for what seemed like hours with men, mostly black.

No one talked. It was a strange sensation, one hundred breathing humans huddled together, silently waiting. Nothing to do, nowhere to sit, just waiting to be called, prodded, and ordered to our next destination.

Finally an alarm sounded and the cell doors opened like floodgates. Bureau guards yelled as they separated us by number, escorting us in groups, herding us into a series of windowless classrooms.

Once inside, we were seated in small uncomfortable metal fold out chairs. A short stout man with a fuzzy black mustache marched through a back door, wired rimmed glasses magnifying his eyes into feline saucers.

"Gentleman," he said, icily. "You are here because you erred, because you dreamed wrong."

"And despite what you might think about the bureau, the recidivist complex is not only a place for punishment," he said.

"Granted we have taken away your freedom, but what you will get in return far exceeds the inconvenience of temporary incarceration."

"In a few minutes a guard will hand you a card listing your dream rehabilitation assignment. I expect you to perform the assigned task with vigor and passion. Those that do will find themselves eligible for early discharge."

"At the complex, we keep people productive so they may learn to think productively. Think about what you might have done to avoid this temporary incarceration, think about your thoughts, consider your dreams to be more than illusions," he said, shaking his fist towards the assembled dreamers.

"We, as human beings, always make the same fatal mistake of giving more import to what we, for example, do with our hands, than what we can think in our minds!"

"You've made that mistake. You think of a dream as a thought, as an idea, as an imperfect story, as only possibility."

"But you must unlearn this prejudice, and our job at the Bureau of Dreams is to make sure you do."

"So simply put, your time at the complex won't be easy, because our job here it to ensure that you don't sleep."

Several grumbled, some simply gasped.

"I know, I know," said the instructor, his fat grubby hands raised. "It sounds cruel, but it is not."

"You will not be denied sleep all the time, but you will find it hard to get peaceful shut eye," he said, chuckling.

"What I want you to take away from this experience is how important it is to be aware of our dreams, how thoughts which seem intangible," he said, "can become real."

"So when you're doing your assigned work and feel tired, think about your thoughts," he said.

"Think about how you think," he said his knotted expression causing his eyes to protrude.

"Think about your dreams."

Shifting his legs like a bow-legged boxer, the speaker glared at us.

"Now many of you are going to experience some of the uncomfortable side effects of sleeplessness."

"Let me assure you all, it can wear on the mind," he continued, pointing his pudgy finger at several men.

"You'll feel disoriented, perhaps dizzy, and almost always agitated."

"But this discomfort can be avoided," he said. "How much sleep you get depends entirely upon you!"

"Those who perform their tasks well, who cooperate with their dream counselor, will find themselves spending plenty of time in the dark room," he said.

"But let me warn you now, uncooperative dreamers, malcontents, and lazy sleepers will find themselves longing for a few minutes of uninterrupted sleep like a thirsty man lost in the desert," he finished, clapping his hands together with the percussive force of a bomb.

"Now, when you receive your assignment cards, please line up across the wall according to the letter at the bottom."

And so as the speaker exited, bureau guards marched in, handing out small white index cards.

On mine the words “Community Surveillance” were written across the bottom, next a letter followed by a number: B4

“All As, in the hall,” the bureau guard shouted. Quickly a dozen men assembled into a line and marched out the door.

“All Bs in the hall,” another guard yelled as another dozen men, myself included, scrambled.

Once outside, the guards checked our index cards, jotting a letter, then a number onto the back of our ID tags.

“Let’s go,” said a guard who along with two other burly escorts with truncheons herded us through a long, gleaming hallway.

As a bureau employee, I had not seen the innards of the complex. I skipped the tours that were available through a bureau employee “enlightenment” program, incurious about a place I never imagined I would be forced to endure.

But now, as we marched in an orderly line down the hall, I wished I had.

Desolate hallways seemed to stretch for miles punctuated only by alcoves that folded into open doorways.

The alcoves were painted. On the left side of the hall, cold black, on the right side, sun orange. They were coded with letters and numbers I could not decipher.

As we passed by the alcoves, I could see inside the sterile classrooms that were filled with men, mostly black, some bleary eyed sitting at a desk writing furiously, others leaning against a wall, reading from a book, raising their heads towards the ceiling like penitents seeking salvation.

At one alcove, a man stumbled into our path, his blood shot eyes filled with tears. He fell backwards, his head rotating like an aimless top. Suddenly a guard grabbed him by the collar, dragging him back inside the alcove, muffling the man’s curses with a thick leather glove.

We were ordered to stop. Next to the alcove on our right was a room that seemed so utterly black light could not escape it. On the other side of the hall, a room so awash with light that it practically blinded me.

"If you aren't feeling motivated," said the guard. "Then take a look at these two rooms," he continued.

"On one side, the dark room, do your job, and you get a few glorious hours in there," the guard continued. "It will be the best sleep you ever had."

"But if you fuck up, and most of you will, then you'll be spending your precious few off hours in what we call the room of unwanted enlightenment," he said, pointing to the room directly across the hall.

The guard nudged us towards the door.

Inside trees of flood lights sat against opposite walls. The blistering beams of dozens of high watt bulbs focused on the center of the room.

Hung from the ceilings were view screens the size of bookcases blasting the dailies with a vengeance. Totem columns of speakers fronted by massive bass cabinets sat on stilts, blaring competing genres of music into a combustible stew of sonic anarchy.

I could see a short, stubby-armed obese man collapsed against the wall, covering his ears in a twisted, strangling embrace. Another, broad shouldered black man lay on the floor, rolling his head from side to side like an uneven metronome. A large, stocky black man with large elf-like ears stood defiantly in the center of room, rocking on the back of his heels, as if he was buffeted by an unrelenting wind.

The sounds and light congealed into an impenetrable wall of discord and anger. Several men were sprawled on the ground, coiled, catatonic, dazed, legs twisted in a chaotic embrace with psychic torture.

As we all watched with horror, an occupant emerged, blood dripping from his ears. A bureau guard dragged him into the hall, slapping him on the back of the head.

"Get moving, Shithead," he yelled, escorting the man to an unseen room perhaps worse than the torture chamber we had just witnessed.

"As you can see, it's in your best interest to keep your metrics positive."

I didn't know what he meant, but I didn't care.

We continued to march past alcoves dead as the city morgue, and alcoves alive with the hum of an active hive.

Finally we were escorted into a room.

Inside we were marshaled into rows until each of us was standing in front of a work station fitted with a view screen and what looked like a ceramic tube protruding from the side.

Ordered to sit on a hard metal stool directly in front of the work station, the guards chained our ankles one by one to braces affixed to the floor.

We waited for several minutes in silence. Suddenly the view screens came to life.

A row of small gray boxes flitted across the screen, filling the entire viewer with murky unblinking squares.

A guard began to read from a laminated index card.

"Errant dreamers, the screen will provide you with detailed instructions on how to perform you tasks," he said in a monotone voice.

"Remember your quota - for first shift you must file fifty citizen complaints in eight hours. If your quota is met, you will receive one hour in the dark room after meal break. If you cannot meet the quota, you will be denied rest and expected to report an additional 10 citizen complaints in the proceeding shift. Please touch the left hand corner of your view screen now."

I touched the top left hand corner.

A set of written instructions appeared on the screen.

Dear Errant Dreamer,

In order to help cure you of odious dreams, you have been assigned to community surveillance shift one.

Your task is relatively simple. Report activity that suggests negativity, destructive behavior, and lack of concern for the welfare of the city.

The surveillance feeds you will see are from some of the most troubled neighborhoods in Balaise.

As you watch, look for events or behaviors which you feel will negatively impact the city and the citizens of Balaise.

Once you have identified an event, touch the box on the screen, and a time coded summary sheet will print out.

Then, with the pen provided, write your reason for reporting the negative occurrence (you may consult the Bureau Behavioral Standards Book attached to your work station), and place it in the pneumatic tube situated on the right side of your work station.

Remember, all reports will be reviewed by bureau dream analysts. If you are found to have made a false report or an unnecessary report, your score for the shift will be halved. For the second offense you will be remanded to the light room for an entire shift.
Your shift begins now.

Suddenly rows of boxes bloomed like algae across the screen, sprouting rectangular monochrome views of street corners, sidewalks, public parks, and bus stops. Arid streetscapes and BBG stands, liquor stores and storefront churches appeared in a collage of Balaise that was active, moving, and frenetic.

For several minutes I simply watched. I never imagined Balaise like this. A sum of its moving parts. Life unraveled through indecipherable narratives, furtive snapshots. It was like seeing a puzzle fully assembled. A pictorial guide to Balaise forged into discrete emblems of decay.

The snapshots were like mini-dramas. A moment in time captured unknowingly, a post card from the ether sent by an unwitting fool.

But as much I just wanted to stare at the screen and absorb the view, thoughts of the bright room turned my mind towards filing reports.

Quickly I scanned the blinking screen searching for bad activity.

I noticed a shot of black men playing dice in the far right hand side of the screen. Four blacks, sitting on a stoop, money spread on the sidewalk. Faces drenched with sweat, jaws taut, collective concentration focused on the uneven sidewalk.

I touched the scene with my fingertip: a bright red box appeared on the screen displaying the word REPORT, framed by a question mark. I touched the screen again to confirm.

The gears of unseen machinery ground softly, casting a light breeze across my hand. A rectangular piece of paper edged over the top of the desk.

The photo captured the men in the throes of gambling. Stamped with a time code, beneath the image several vertical lines headed with the word "explanation" were aligned underneath.

Quickly I wrote a synopsis in bureau speak, folding the complaint inside the aluminum tube. Once inside the pod, a red button flashed "report" until I pushed it. The tube was sucked into a vacuum like a metallic lizard's tongue, disappearing in an instant.

One down, but dozens more to go.

I frantically scanned the screen for new violations. The views refreshed with ferocious regularity.

Again I had to force myself to focus. Mesmerized by the dozens of scenes unfolding and then evaporating like miniature dreams, the thought of writing reports seemed like a nuisance. Instead I wished to simply watch the world unfold.

Why couldn't I just observe? If I touched my finger to the screen, my action would end the intoxicating scenery of unscripted life. Why send a Bureau Guard to undo the spontaneity? Why end the mini-dramas privy only to me?

This thought weighed on my mind as I watched a young black couple loiter on a corner corralling each other into an awkward embrace. Then a young black mother pushed a stroller with three small toddlers clinging to her overcoat, mounting the stairs of a bus, children in tow. A group of young boys speeding through an alley on makeshift bicycles darted in and out of view of a camera, leaving contrails of pixels in their wake.

After the screen refreshed, the couple reappeared still engaged in the unwieldy dance. The woman turned and twisted like a ballerina, while the man grasped her shoulders. Then she spun around suddenly, dropping onto his chest like an old doll. Was it an embrace, or had he co-opted her into his arms by force?

Without hesitation, I touched the screen. The snapshot printed.

"About assault," I wrote at the bottom before placing it in the pneumatic tube.

Two down, twenty to go.

For at least a half an hour I watched the screen unblinkingly. Snapshots appeared, tantalizing dramas that seemed to dance on the edge of infraction. A black man weaved in a serpentine path along a sidewalk, a bottle hidden in a brown paper bag tucked under his arm like a football.

A black woman sprinted out of a corner store, tossing what looked like packages of cigarettes to outreaching hands lined along a desolate back alley.

A black teenager darted across the screen holding an unseen object tightly in his hand. Soon thereafter another boy followed, he too seemingly carrying something in his hand.

But while the dozens of snapshots offered a nearly god like view of the city, the limitations of the lens made it difficult to lift my hand. Did the woman steal the cigarettes? Was the man stumbling down the street drunk? What was the young man doing? How would I know?

Still, despite my doubts, I touched the screens. What else could I do? Yes the bureau would dock my score if I erred, but it seemed unlikely the deputy major deployed hundreds of cameras throughout the city, constructed a complex remand center, and employed thousands of bureau workers just to be lenient. The bureau analysts tasked with reviewing my reports probably had quotas too.

So I began to report any activity that seemed less than innocuous, any action that suggested even a hint of wrong doing. By simply selecting a scene that seemed suspicious, and using the broad definitions of violations made available by the bureau, it only took me an hour to meet and then surpass my quota.

It was a strange feeling of power that belied the chains coiled around my ankles. I could see everything unfold at once. The screens blinked like obedient children. The stories hidden inside terminal shadows were now on display.

I began to run my hand across the monitor with a new found passion, enlarging scenes with the agility of a pianist. It was easy to judge, and even more empowering to pass judgment. Ambivalent infractions soon became extensions of my paranoid imaginings, my former ambivalence eradicated by surety of an all seeing eye. What I believed to be wrong became just that with the touch of a hand.

While I scribbled away furiously, I barely noticed the two behemoth bureau guards suddenly posted on either side of my work station.

Dressed in dark suits the size of bedspreads, the angular jawed linebackers stood and stared. Unflinching bulwarks out of place in the sterile classroom filled with dreamers chained to the floor.

I continued monitoring the screen, more concerned about keeping up with my quota then their presence.

But then I felt a hand on my shoulder, a hand that lingered while several fingers nestled under my triceps, pinching seams of skin together like a suture.

I did not turn around. The buzz of the machines spitting out reports continued. The other detainees in the room remained engrossed in their work.

Suddenly the grip on my shoulder relaxed. The hand slid slowly down my back.

A man wearing a military uniform sidled in front of my desk, ducking his shoulders until we were face to face.

It was the deputy major.

"So this is the troublemaker," he said, his light blue enamel eyes murky and unyielding.

Taking a seat in a fold-out chair dropped next to my desk, the deputy major's thick black hair looked disoriented and wild, his trademark sideburns flustered and unwieldy.

"This is the man that single-handedly tried to embarrass the bureau and me," he said.

"I had to see you in person," he said softly.

The deputy major shifted in his chair, unbuttoning the embroidered clasp of a black leather collar.

"A traitor is a stubborn creature, an unbending personality," he said.

"No matter the evidence against him, no matter the pain of self-inflicted wounds, a traitor will not relent until he himself is destroyed," he continued.

"I understand traitors," he said, plucking a gold cigarette lighter from his breast pocket and waving it in the air.

"Do you know what motivates a traitor?" the deputy major asked.

But I could not answer. I had never met the deputy, only watched him from a distant chair in an auditorium. Or listened to his rich baritone voice on the nightlies. And now I was a few inches from his face.

I was speechless.

"Do you know what motivates a traitor?" he repeated, snapping his fingers at a guard, who responded by producing a cigarette.

"No," I finally replied.

"Jealousy," he snapped. "Pure, and simply jealousy."

"Seems obvious, doesn't it?" he added. "But the motives of the traitor are the least best understood in all of politics."

"A traitor betrays because great leadership has an Achilles heel," he said.

"That is, when a great leader emerges, there's little room for others," he continued. "The pathological, the insane, the demented, and worst of all the incapable, all plot against the leader because they are jealous."

"I didn't know, "I replied.

"Maybe," he replied. "But I would imagine if you examined your motives, it would eventually become clear, that you are simply jealous of me."

The deputy major smiled, his sparkling white teeth aligned in perfect symmetry.

"I'm sure you've spent countless hours wishing the bureau was your idea," he said. "Or thinking that if you were running it, how much more improved Balaise would be."

"Or perhaps hoping that your relatively obscure position as a former recorder of waivers was higher profile. A job worthy of coverage by the tablets," he paused, waiting for me to respond.

"I never really thought about it."

The deputy major laughed, springing out of his chair, wrapping his arm around my neck.

"That's why you're a traitor," he exclaimed. "You never considered the actual possibility that your motives were completely selfish! It astounds me."

Sitting down again, the deputy major quietly stewed, rubbing his chin, rolling his eyes, before speaking again.

"Let me say this before I act," he continued. "I don't forgive you, but I also don't blame you."

"The miracle of Balaise's renaissance belongs to all the people, but the credit belongs solely to me," he continued.

"And I'm sure that is a difficult fact for any man, anyone with just an ounce of ambition to accept."

"Power, acclaim, and a whole lot of ass," he said, chuckling. "But I can't say I blame you," he finished, rising from the chair, waving to a body guard.

"Unfortunately your treachery also forces my hand," he continued. "As much I was would like you to participate in this wonderful healing program we provide to errant dreamers, I've chosen to terminate your rehabilitation for the moment to ensure that you don't come back and bite me in the ass."

Snapping his fingers, a bureau guard quickly unchained my feet.

"The bright room is where you'll stay, until you acknowledge your self destructive tendencies."

"I'm sorry," he added. "But my deputies wanted to kill you."

I didn't know what to say. I would have admitted to any crime simply to avoid the bright room. But it seemed clear the deputy major was not interested in a confession.

"Silent, aren't we?" he said as a bodyguard placed a coat over his shoulders.

"Don't think I'm not impressed," he finished, smiling as the guard dragged me out of the room.

"Wait," he said, snapping his fingers. The guards held my body like a kite, slowly edging me closer to the deputy major.

"If you ever get out of here, which I doubt you will," the deputy major said. "Make sure you remind Jasmine Brown about our little fuck session in the basement of city hall."

"I'm sure she'll remember it, I know I do!" he exclaimed, bellowing until his body convulsed into hiccups that sounded like laughter. "She was quite a fuck, a real special piece of ass," he added, clapping his hands like a punch-drunk seal.

"She was quite a fuck," was all I heard as the guards shoved me down the hall.

En route to the bright room, I wondered. Was the deputy major right? Was I jealous? And had he really fucked Jasmine Brown?

If he had, I was definitely jealous.

But his analysis of my motives became less interesting as I approached the bright room.

Nearing the bureau's best version of a torture chamber, my greatest fear was losing my composure. I didn't want the story of the ex-recorder of waivers pleading for mercy to become bureau lore, or grist for Reel's lunchtime mill.

Still when the alcove appeared, my knees began to falter.

"How long?" I asked the smiling guard.

"As long as the deputy major wants," he said.

Shoved past the alcove and through the door, the symphonic blast of light and sound was worse than I had imagined.

Like an avalanche of ether poured into my skull, the dual onslaught of both intense sound and scalding light was almost immediately unbearable.

I stumbled around, groping for a wall. The flood-lights followed my every movement, vengeful stars intent on scratching my corneas like an angry cat.

Meanwhile the swell of overwhelming grinding metal music, caustic voice-overs, and putrid jingles congealed into a vortex of mind-numbing noise. As much as the light impeded me from seeing, the toxic sounds made it impossible to move without falling, stumbling, or crawling along the ground.

I closed my eyes, wrapping my arms around my head in an awkward self-embrace.

But it didn't help. The light was so intense and the sound so unrelenting I felt like I was drowning in an insanely frenetic fish bowl.

Still I sat huddled the corner of the room, hoping I could remain calm, composed, even to bear it with a bit of dignity.

Presently someone tapped me on the shoulder. Reluctant to open my eyes, I ignored it.

But then the shoulder tap turned into a take-down, and I was suddenly on my back looking up.

A man with dark hair wearing black goggles and pair of headphones smiled, extending his hand. At first I didn't recognize him, but as my eyes adjusted to the burning flood of stigmatic light, I realized I was looking at the deputy major.

He lifted me off the floor, thrusting me against the wall. Pulling a pair of cone-shaped headphones out from under his embroidered overcoat, he deftly placed them on my head, activating a microphone that delivered his voice into the inner canals of my ear.

"This is amazing, isn't it," he said, his voice crackling electric, buffeted by a wave of static in the headphones.

I didn't answer.

"We've been tweaking the room for awhile, but I really think it's finally perfect."

"I would agree," I replied.

"Don't worry, you won't be in here forever," he said.

"But I just wanted to know what you thought," he added. "Total mind fuck, right?"

"Right."

"So next time, maybe, you'll think twice about fucking with me, right?" he said, pinching my cheek.

"Yes," I nodded. "Now can I leave?"

"Hell no, I want to make sure you got the message loud and clear," he said, laughing.

"I got it."

"We'll see," he answered.

The deputy major ripped the headphones off my skull, the cool oasis of near silence shattered by the onslaught of pre-programmed mayhem.

He patted me on the shoulder, turned, and walked into the glow of the unforgiving sun.

The brief respite from the onslaught of noise only made the pain worse. I could barely keep myself from screaming, raging at the sound, toppling the view-screens, and railing against the floodlights.

Out of the corner of my eye, I saw a fellow inmate grappling with a totem column of speakers that nearly touched the ceiling. His bloodied hands gripped the massive towers, rocking them back and forth, until the entire stack bent like an upended tree.

Instantly he was set upon by a posse of guards. They beat him savagely, stomping his face and kicking his ribs while the he flailed like a rabid dog.

I embraced the wall, trying to stem the unrelenting sonic assault by placing my right ear against it.

I groped for crevices, fingered the small indentations, hoping to find a hole big enough to swallow me.

But it was futile, the wall was unforgiving. My senses were now ablaze.

I started to panic. The waves of thunder and lightening grew indistinguishable. The light became nuclear, the sound catastrophic.

Dropping to the floor, I pulled my knees into my chest, joining my fellow inmates who also went fetal, dotting the room like giant hermit crabs.

I lay on the floor for seconds, minutes or hours, I do not know. The pain froze time, embalming my senses, obliterating any thought other than now.

I felt tears stream down my cheeks. I couldn't concede the pain, or even remember why it hurt. But immersed in the seething barrel of needles, helplessness overwhelmed me. I begged the floor for mercy, unleashing a violent scream that only added to my misery.

And that is the way I stayed for what seemed like hours: a catatonic, immobile, twitching, epileptic baby.

Until I felt a hand grasp my by the collar, and drag me across the floor.

I did not fight back. I couldn't. But the hand continued to pull me like I was a stubborn corpse. Soon I was out the door and through the alcove.

"Get up, don't say a word, and follow-me."

I was lifted me off the ground. A black man the size of a freezer dressed in bureau uniform grasped me by the shoulders, righting my body with superhuman strength.

"Follow me," he repeated, slapping me across the brow.

I felt like a child ejected from the womb of hell.

My legs wobbled, my knees shook, my hands trembled and my eyes filled with tears.

"Jesus," he said, turning around, shaking me.

"You need to man up, we don't have much time."

His face was immediately familiar. Even through vision blurred by tears, I recognized him.

“Don’t say a fucking word, just follow and stay quiet,” he snapped.

Dressed in full bureau regalia, one of Brown’s bodyguards led me down the hall.

We passed gangs of errant dreamers en route to assignments, strung out sleepers, stumbling catatonic bearing medic patches, bloodshot eyes crimson and bloated.

We passed classrooms binging on fluorescence. Steady workers plying at unseen keyboards. Bowed heads immersed in the angular glow of a view screen. Bureau supervisors strutting in front of dreamers, legs fastened to the floor.

Waves of errant dreamers pushed us against the wall, an endless mass of turbulent bodies. Marching in serpentine lines. Faces masked by shame.

Finally we reached a large oval portal.

“Do what I say, and don’t ask any questions,” he said, gripping my arm until it turned blue.

“I’m going to throw you out the window,” he said. “Don’t panic, just stay loose.”

I would have protested if I had the strength.

Wrapping his hand in his bureau jacket, the bodyguard plunged his fist through the portal. Shattered glass filled the hallway as a screeching alarm enveloped the complex.

Quickly the bodyguard wrapped his arms around my chest. With a violent jerk, he righted my body parallel to the floor. Stepping back several yards from the portal, he took a running start before thrusting me through the hole like a battering ram.

The entire act seemed supernatural. One second I was standing upright, the next I was hurtling through the air, dropping like a log to an unseen end.

As I plunged towards the ground, I unleashed a primal scream interrupted by a back-breaking fall into a pile of garbage.

A fountain of confetti exploded. I sank into the heap of trash like a felled corpse. Buried under a paper fold of internal office memos and discarded file folders, I lay still.

Suddenly the pile of garbage began to move. Through the layers of trash, I watched the backside of the complex disappear, a high pitched squeal of the siren still ringing.

Tremors of pain radiated up my spine. But the quiet comfort of an improvised paper nest lulled me into deep, dreamless sleep.

"Wake up, Bureau Boy,"

Jasmine stood over my cot, a cigarette dangling from her mouth.

"You are one lucky nigger," she laughed.

The room looked smaller, my cot less comfortable.

"How the hell did you end up in the complex?"
"Bad luck, I guess."
"Get dressed and join us," she ordered, exiting the room.

I changed into a white t-shirt laid across the turn-table next to my bed.

Jasmine and her followers sat quietly in the ante room, arranged around the table like a council of elders.

"I failed," I said before sitting down.

"Even though everything you thought was true was in fact true," I continued. "It didn't matter."

"No one wants the story," I added.

"No one wants a story that contradicts their own," Brown replied.

Suddenly she began to laugh, her cohorts joining in until the whole room turned riotous.

"I don't get it. What's so fucking funny?" I asked, as Brown continued to laugh.

"You, you're funny," she replied. "You found the men, survived the complex, and now you're worried because no one wanted your fucked-up story."

Jasmine snapped her fingers. A bodyguard rose from his chair, disappearing behind a black door. Minutes later he returned with a black manual typewriter, unceremoniously dropping it in front of me.

"What's this?"
"What does it look like?"

It was old, worn keys, a dusty ink tape, nicks and cuts marred the iron casing.

"What do you want me to do?"

Jasmine chuckled.

"Your little sojourn didn't wise you up."
"Oh, it did."

"Then don't ask, just write."
"Write?"

A bottle of brandy slid across the table. Brown quickly poured a shot into a glass, passing it to her bodyguard who thrust it in front of me.

"Take a sip, and then write about what you saw."

I tilted the glass. The brandy was brown and murky.

"I'm not a writer."
"Jesus, just tell the fucking story. You don't need permission to remember, do you?"

I acknowledged Brown's admonishment by downing the glass.

"I can't write."

Brown stood up, placed her hands on the table, all the while staring me down like she was going to vanquish me.

"I didn't rescue your ass from the complex just to have you tell me what you can't do," she said.

"Now sit yourself down at that typewriter and tell the goddam story, or I'll have my men deliver you back to the complex C-O-D."

"Understood?"
"Yes," I replied.

I touched the typewriter. A blank piece of white paper sat ready.

The room was silent, all eyes upon me. Brewing cigarette smoke, the scent of brandy.

The smell of the complex lingered. The institutional after-wash, the stench of unclean bodies, the dreamless sleep of the bright room.

"What are you waiting for?" Brown asked.
"I'm thinking"
"You're done thinking," she snapped. "Just write."

I placed my hands across the keys, exhaled slowly, and began to type.

I work for the bureau of dreams in the city of Balaise.

I am a reviewer of waivers assigned to district four, sector three.

Stephen Janis is an award winning investigative reporter who has covered crime and corruption in Baltimore City.

As a staff writer for The Baltimore Examiner (and one of only a handful who worked at the paper for its entire existence) he won a Maryland Delaware D.C. Press Association award in 2008 for investigative reporting on the high rate of unsolved murders in Baltimore, and a 2009 award for best series of his articles on the high number of unsolved deaths of prostitutes.

Covering City Hall and crime, Janis revealed that a city parking agent was writing fake tickets, leading to an ongoing investigation by Baltimore City Inspector General Hilton Green. In 2007, Janis won an award from the Baltimore Chapter of the NAACP for his coverage of issues affecting the black community. His investigative series on the controversial suicide ruling in the death of Baltimore political activist Robert Clay lead to an investigation by the Baltimore Inspector General, who recommended the justice department re-open the case.

Prior to joining The Examiner, Janis was a contributing writer for the Baltimore City Paper. He is an instructor at The Johns Hopkins School of Communications and Contemporary Society in Washington, D.C. The New York City native is a graduate of Hamilton College.

Novelzine published Janis' first book, Orange: The Diary of an Urban Surrealist in the February 2009.

Made in United States
North Haven, CT
11 October 2024